Praise for Tonya Kappes

"Full of wit, humor and colorful characters, Tonya Kappes delivers a fun, fast-paced story that will leave you hooked!" Bestselling Author, Jane Porter

"Fun, fresh, and flirty, Carpe Bead 'Em is the perfect read on a hot summer day. Tonya Kappes' voice shines in her debut novel." Author Heather Webber

"I loved how Tonya Kappes was able to bring her characters to life." Coffee Table Reviews

With laugh out loud scenes and can't put it down suspense A Charming Crime is the perfect read for summer you get a little bit of everything but romance. Forgetthehousework blog

"A Ghostly Undertaking is hauntingly good read with authentic Southern charm." Heather Blake

Also by Tonya Kappes

Women's Fiction

Carpe Bead 'em

Olivia Davis Paranormal Mystery Series

Splitsville.com

Color Me A Crime

Magical Cures Mystery Series

A Charming Crime

A Charming Cure

A Charming Potion

A Charming Wish

A Charming Spell

Grandberry Falls Series

The Ladybug Jinx

Happy New Life

A Superstitious Christmas

Never Tell Your Dreams

A Divorced Diva Beading Mystery Series

A Bead of Doubt Short Story

Strung Out To Die

A

Charming Spell

A Magical Cures Mysteries

Tonya Kappes

Acknowledgments

This is for all the people who have supported me and encouraged me on this crazy, dream journey and believing in my imagination and ability to bring to out on the page. You know who you are.

Xo

Chapter One

"June, June, wake up." My head bobbled back and forth on my pillow, because my neighbor, Oscar Park, was shaking the crap out of my arm.

"Shh…" I mumbled with my eyes shut tight, even though seeing my blue-eyed, black-haired hunky neighbor was a much more pleasant sight then my dark eyelids.

"You'll wake Darla."

Darla Heal. My mom.

Darla was not like every other mom. She was, well…different. She owned and operated A Dose of Darla, a booth at our local flea market in Locust Grove, Kentucky, where she sold her own versions of homeopathic cures that she concocted in the basement of our small Cape Cod home.

And Oscar…well, he was a different story. Oscar and I had a lot of similarities. He was raised by his Uncle Jordan after his parents were killed in a tragic car wreck, while I was raised by my mother after my police officer father got killed in the line of duty.

Anyway, Oscar always had a habit of sneaking into my room at night, but not without my all-time favorite treat, which Darla didn't allow me to have, Ding Dongs.

"I've got a present for you." Oscar waved his temptation underneath my nose. I didn't have to open my eyes to know it was my favorite chocolaty treat.

Beep, beep, beep. My alarm woke me up, bringing me to my current situation.

"No, no, no." I begged and reached over to tap the snooze button. Mr. Prince Charming was curled up on my pillow, unaffected by the beeping hunk of junk. "I was having the best dream too."

I brushed my bangs out of my eyes so I could see the clock. I had a few more minutes, so I wiggled back under my covers. I closed my eyes, trying to remember the dream, but it only brought back memories, some of which I would like to forget.

Oscar Park and I had come a long way since those days of him sneaking into my bedroom window. Especially now since I lived in Whispering Falls, Kentucky and he was living back in Locust Grove.

Ah. . .the good old days, I sighed and closed my eyes.

The good old days weren't that long ago. Now, everything had changed.

Chapter Two

Knock, knock, knock. My heart nearly leapt out of my chest when I heard someone at my front door. Maybe my dream was coming true.

"I guess we aren't going to get to snooze." Madame Torres, my cynical crystal ball, glowed red with swirling gold flecks. It was a sure sign she was not happy, which was not a great way to start my day.

"No, I guess not." I was sure my dream was just wishful thinking that Oscar hadn't given up his spiritual powers and any memories of me being a spiritualist, just so he could help me out in the sticky situation I was in at the time.

I threw the covers off me. The cold air hit me, sending a chill across my arms.

Rowl, rowl. Mr. Prince Charming, my fairy god-cat, growled when my covers landed on top of him.

"Oops." I laughed and peeled them back. His white-as-snow fur was sticking up from a little static electricity.

Bang, bang, bang. The gentle knocking had turned into an angry "answer your door now" knock.

"I'm coming!" I screamed, reaching for a sweatshirt that didn't match my pajama bottoms, but it was going to have to work.

I wasn't going to let anyone ruin my day. It was going to be great! After all, tonight was the village council meeting and my first time as the newly elected Village President.

Bang, bang, bang.

Geez. When did everyone get in such a hurry? I walked down the hall, flipping on light switches as I went.

"This better be important and you had better have brought me a coffee," I warned before I swung the door open.

"June," Alexelrod Primose, Whispering Falls' only realtor pushed past me without an invitation to enter. "You have to stop the sale of the old building that is next to Bella's Baubles."

He stood about five-foot-eight with his round-brimmed hat resting on his head. It dawned on me that I had never seen him without his hat or his long black overcoat.

Alexelrod swung his briefcase in the direction of my kitchen table and proceeded to follow in that direction as if the briefcase was dragging him along. "We need to discuss this."

"I…" My hand was still on the door handle. Gently, I closed it behind me and crossed my arms in front of me. "It's early. Can we discuss this later?"

"Later? Absolutely not." His voice was firm and final. He slammed the briefcase on the table. "This could change how Whispering Falls does business…*forever*." Lines formed around his deep-set worried brown eyes.

"Forever is a long time." I didn't want to get sucked into a long debate over whether or not a new shop was going to destroy Whispering Falls. My intuition, which happened to be one of my spiritual gifts, never failed me. It wasn't warning me at this moment, which meant that this conversation could wait. At least until I had my first or third cup of coffee. "What kind of shop is going in there anyway?"

Not everything had been transferred over to me from Isadora Solstice, the last Whispering Falls Village President. Any deals made with new shop owners before last week was all her doing. We had plans to catch up before the meeting tonight to discuss anything new…like this.

I walked over to the sink and looked out the window overlooking the meadow that bordered the village. I was lucky to have a house nestled on a little hill that overlooked the magical city I called home.

The lush green grass was beautiful as it rolled down to the city. The sun was just making its first appearance overtop the mountains that surrounded Whispering Falls, putting off a faint light.

"A bookstore of all things." *Thump!* Alexelrod's beat his fist, causing the briefcase to burst open. Papers flew out all over the place.

Alexelrod didn't care. He was deep in the large black case tossing out even more papers on the table. Mr. Prince Charming was perched on the couch behind the table in my family room.

Ugh. Inwardly I cringed. Mr. Prince Charming had his back leg stuck straight up in the air as he bathed himself. That meant that I was going to have to clean the fur off my beautiful orange couch when he was finished.

"A bookstore?" I questioned with an escalated voice. "I love books!"

"You can't be serious!"

"Dead serious." This entire conversation was giving me a headache and dose of liquid happiness was exactly what I needed. My new single-cup coffee maker was perfect for me. I picked out Java Jolt. That sounded perfect. "Would you like a cup of coffee?"

"How could you even *think* about coffee when this is of the utmost importance? Urgent!" His eyes narrowed as he pumped his fist in the air.

"Nothing is urgent at this time of the morning." Well…almost nothing. The clock on the stove read six am.

I had set my alarm early because I wanted to get to my shop, A Charming Cure, a couple of hours before it opened. There was a potion I needed to work on that was of the *utmost* importance. A spell to get Oscar's memory back. His memory of why I had moved to Whispering Falls.

I sat in the chair next to Alexelrod and pushed his papers toward him.

"I understand this is important to you." I had to make him feel somewhat comfortable coming to me since I was the Village President. "And it just so happens that we are having a village meeting tonight where you can discuss these issues with the community leaders."

He grabbed the papers. They wrinkled as he wadded them up and threw them back in the briefcase before he slammed it shut and locked it up.

"Good day, Madame President." He stood up, tilted his head, and bee-lined it to the door, his lips pursed tightly.

"Alexelrod, please understand that if I allow one person to come into my home and suggest things for the community, then everyone will want to." There had to be a line drawn somewhere. I just didn't know where.

Obviously, Alexelrod had no interest in what I was saying. He opened the door, and without turning back around, slammed it behind him, almost catching Mr. Prince Charming's tail as he darted through right behind Alexelrod.

"Where are you going?" I shouted toward the door, before glancing out the window.

Mr. Prince Charming didn't turn around either. He darted down the hill. I watched until his tail danced out of sight.

Chapter Three

A few minutes later, I was ready to tackle the day. I headed down the hill with Madame Torres deep in my bag and my cell phone in my back pocket.

A Charming Cure was located at the far end of Main Street on the right side of the road next to A Cleansing Spirit Spa and across the street from the Whispering Hills Police Station. That is where I used to see Oscar every day until he made the worst decision of his life.

He denounced his spiritual heritage to save me from a little incident I was accused of doing – which I didn't do and had to prove. Regardless, Oscar lost his powers and his memory of why we had both moved to Whispering Falls. Now he was a police officer in Locust Grove with no memory of ever living in Whispering Falls or anything we had done here.

He thought I moved here to open a brick-and-mortar store instead of staying in the flea market booth.

The village was quiet, even though I knew Eloise Sandlewood had already walked the streets a few hours before, waving her incense burner in and out of every shop gate to bring fortune, health, and wealth to the community, just as she did every morning.

There was a faint light coming from the opposite direction on Main Street from Wicked Good Bakery. That was the first shop on the right when visitors drove in. Everyone loved the baked goods that Raven Mortimer created with her magical hands. I was sure if I stopped for a brief moment and took in a fresh breath of air, I'd smell Raven's baked goodies.

But not today. There wasn't time to dilly-dally. I had to get started on my cure that I could slip into Oscar's food

to bring back his memory and our newly blossoming
romance.

The awnings over each shop flapped in the morning
wind. I glanced around, looking at each shop to make sure
there wasn't any funny business going on. All the stores
had a beautifully ornamented gate that opened up into the
pathway leading up to a shop door, but they all seemed to
be locked tight.

Creak, creak. The wooden sign that hung on the
wrought-iron post outside of the shop and read A Charming
Cure, slowly swung back and forth on the hinges.

Mr. Prince Charming ran up out of nowhere doing his
signature figure-eight move around my ankles and between
my legs. He knew when my gut was unsettled and was
there to protect me each and every time. This time was no
different. My stomach gurgled with nerves.

"I'm fine." I bent down and rubbed my hand along his
body as he arched to my touch. "I'm sure I'm just nervous
about the ceremony, not to mention Oscar."

I stood up and bit my lip before taking one more
glance around Main Street. Alexelrod's plea was still
swirling in my head, making me doubt the cautious feeling
that was churning inside as I was about to take the reins as
Village President.

Shaking off the notion that something was wrong, Mr.
Prince Charming and I unlocked the front gate and headed
up the path to the shop. The purple and white wisteria vine
grew beautifully around the two windows, one on either
side of the door.

A Charming Cure was everything that Darla and I had
dreamed of. I only wished she were here to help.

"Let's get to work." I unlocked the door and stepped
inside. Mr. Prince Charming darted in and took his spot on

the counter next to the cash register where he normally sat most of the day.

I set my bag on the stool that butted up to the counter and took Madame Torres out and put her on her usual spot on the counter. She did like sitting there watching the customers as they came in and out all day. Not to mention, she gets her kicks from how they are in "awe" over her because they think she's some sort of decoration.

I walked throughout the shop, turning on all the little table lights, illuminating the inside. Several small round tables dotted the inside of the shop, covered in beautiful red tablecloths. Each table held different potion bottles for different cures.

Flipping on my cauldron – that was hidden from the public behind a small partition on the counter – I walked back to the shelf where I kept all the ingredients I use for my special cures. Tapping each one, I read their names out loud, trying to tap into my intuition. "Belladonna, Ferrum Phos, Sepia, Natrum Mur, Valerian Root."

My finger warmed when I touched the Valerian Root, which was my intuition telling me to pick that ingredient.

"You've never failed me yet." I said, referring to my spiritual gift of intuition. Gingerly, I picked up the hourglass bottle with the pink roses etched into the hazy glass that I kept the root in.

After grabbing a few extra ingredients, for good measure of course, I placed them all on the counter.

Tourists that shopped in the stores in Whispering Falls knew there was something mysterious about our small village, but they couldn't exactly tell you what it was. There was magic at every turn. Every shop owner was a spiritualist and used their "gift" in their stores.

As gifts go, there was no way I could speak for every shop owner in Whispering Falls, but in A Charming Cure I created and sold homeopathic cures.

For instance, some of my clients believe they are coming to get a cure for a bad case of indigestion, but in reality, they might have a broken heart or financial problems. After being in their presence, my intuition gift kicks in and lets me know exactly what cure they *really* need. If they follow my instructions to a tee, their real problems will be gone.

Today...I had problems of my own.

The cauldron roiled at a low boil. With a couple sprinkles of Sage, a dash of Ledum, and a pinch of Valerian Root, the substance turned orange. Rose-colored bubbles popped in the air like little fireworks.

I closed my eyes and held my hands over the swirling liquid. Moving my hands in slow circles, I whispered, "I am peaceful, I am strong. Though dark may seem so long. For day must follow every night. Everything is all right. I am always safe from harm. The Order of Elders holds me in their arms."

"There is not much we can do for you." Mary Ellen levitated in the air with her arms crossed before she floated down and landed on her cute leopard-print cowboy boots. Her long black hair hung over each shoulder in braids.

"There has to be something." I bit the side of my lip. I wondered if I was ever going to get used to the comings and goings of all the Marys, known as the Elders. They were going to be around for a while since I was appointed the new Village President. That was part of their job. To make sure the transition went smoothly.

There were three elders: Mary Lynn, Mary Sue, and Mary Ellen. They were equivalent to the President of the United States in the spiritualist world. The Village

Presidents (me) are like the governors of the spiritual communities.

"I'm having a bit of a panic attack." I dipped the ladle into the cauldron and took a small sip of the liquid. My nose curled. "Eww." I shook my head like it was going to get rid of the bitter taste.

"Is it the first meeting as Village President that is bothering you or…" She adjusted her emerald green belt that accented her tiny waist.

"Or what?"

"Or…" Her eyes narrowed, casting a shadow down her cheeks. "Is it Oscar Park you are concerned with?"

"Both." I sighed, heavily. The thought of being in charge of a community made my head hurt. That Oscar Park had lost all of his spiritual powers and memory of ever having lived in Whispering Falls because of me, made my entire body hurt. Especially my heart.

"He made the decision to stop being a spiritualist to help you."

"He did it without asking me first."

"He is a big boy." Mary Ellen tossed a braid over her shoulder. "And a mighty fine specimen at that."

I eyed her, letting her know that I didn't like her comment.

"What is the potion for?" Mary Ellen changed the subject and peeked into the cauldron. She looked at me with a cautious eye.

Did she know what I was up to? I'd take my chance and *lie.*

"I need something to settle my nerves." The bitter taste still lingered in my mouth. I grabbed the little jar of honey off the shelf and squirted a little in the cauldron. Stirring the mixture I said, "This should do the trick."

Normally, I didn't like to do chants in front of people. This wasn't a normal situation. Mary Ellen wasn't leaving and I had limited time before the shop opened.

It was already eight thirty and there was only a half hour until it was time to open.

With my hands back over the cauldron, I waved them back and forth, chanting, ""I am peaceful, I am strong. Though dark may seem so long. For day must follow every night. Everything is all right. I am always safe from harm. The Order of Elders holds me in their arms."

The roiling mix came to an abrupt stop, letting me know it was ready.

"That doesn't look like any ole calming potion to me." Mary Ellen's brows rose significantly. She stuck her finger in the hot mixture. The entire pot solidified like concrete causing my cauldron to shatter into pieces all over the counter and floor. "Ha! I knew it!"

"My cauldron!" I cried as I dropped to the ground to pick up the pieces that had crashed to the floor. Luckily, what was left was mostly on the counter.

"June Heal," Mary Ellen stated sharply as she floated in the space between my head and the ceiling and waved a wand over me, "consider yourself on probation! You cannot go against the elders and their rulings. Oscar Park's powers were taken away once and for all!"

She snapped her fingers. A puff of pink smoke filled the air before Mary Ellen disappeared.

Cough, cough. I put my hand over my mouth careful not to breathe in the pink smoke. I rushed over to the window and pushed it up to let in some fresh air. I couldn't let the customers think I had a batch of bad cures brewing.

"Probation? Whatever!" I fanned the air as I made my way back to the counter, but stopped when I heard an unfamiliar sound in Whispering Falls.

Construction.

I went back to the window and looked across the street. There was a woman wearing a pair of jeans with a white tight-fitting sweater and black wedge sandals. Her honey-blond hair tumbled down her back in beautiful loose curls. She was pointing something out to the man in the hardhat standing next to her. He used all his might to hammer something into the brick. When he was finished, they stood back and admired the sign.

"Ever After Books." I smiled at the name. It was a very enchanting name and the store would certainly draw the tourists.

I pulled back when the woman turned my way and looked directly at A Charming Cure, and more specifically, at me.

I flipped the sign to OPEN, taking a quick peek across the street.

The woman was gone, but the crew was still there putting the awning over the door as the final touch. It rolled down in place, right above the windows.

"Ever After Books." The purple lettering stood out on the khaki-colored canvas.

"Ophelia Biblio: five-foot five-inches with curly honey-blond hair. Very nice." Madame Torres read off the new owner's stats. "From a spiritualist community in Ohio. Single and ready to mingle."

"Single and what?" I snickered at Madame Torres's sense of humor. She was sometimes off-handed, but at other times very entertaining.

"That is what her old match profile said." Madame Torres's globe glowed with the Make-Me-A-Match dating site for spiritualists. Something I had recently heard about, but had no interest in using.

Apparently it was the newest rage in the spiritual world. After all, it was hard to meet someone that was compatible. You can't put a palm reader with an astrologer. They'd fight over the sun, moon, and stars all of the time. Generally, we spiritualists were far too busy trying to help others instead of taking care of our own needs.

The bell ding-donged over the door bringing me out of my thoughts.

"Good morning." Constance Karima greeted me when she walked in with Patience, her twin, not too far behind.

"Speaking of our needs," Madame Torres mumbled. "You'd better snag you a new man or get on Make-Me-A-Match before you turn out like those two old spiritualist spinsters." Madame Torres's eyes filled the globe. "*Alone.*"

"Shh…" I warned Madame Torres to be quiet. She wasn't the type of crystal ball that could help you out when you needed her to and be silent until you did. She was far too opinionated for that and she didn't care who heard her.

"Why?" Constance Karima swayed back and forth on her small feet in her pointy black boots. Her black housecoat hung to her ankles. She picked at her short grey hair. Patience mimicked her sister's every move.

"Why?" I asked back a bit confused.

"You told me to shush." Constance narrowed her eyes, casting a shadow down her puffed up cheeks. She eased over and took a good look at the mess from the busted up cauldron.

"Yes, mm, hmm, shh." Patience had a habit of repeating her sister.

"Oh, I'm sorry. I was talking to Mr. Prince Charming." I lied.

Growl. Mr. Prince Charming let me know his dislike for my comment. On my way over to grab my apron off the hook, I ran my hand down his back to make him happier. *Purrr, purr.*

I looked at the mess with great sadness. There wasn't going to be any cure making today or for a while, until I could purchase a new cauldron. That wouldn't be until I could make it to Wands, Potions, and Beyond. Unfortunately, it wasn't going to be anytime soon, since it was at Hidden Hall A Spiritualist University, my alma mater and where my Aunt Helena was the Dean.

It had been awhile since I had seen her and there were a lot of questions I needed to ask. Even though she was a Fairiwick, she did dabble a bit in the unknown, which was just what I needed to find a cure for Oscar.

I smacked the broom on the floor when I realized Aunt Helena could help me with Oscar.

"June Heal, what is wrong with you today?" Constance grabbed Patience's arm and dragged her toward the door. "We are leaving."

"Wait!" I hollered after her after my odd behavior scared them. I didn't want them spreading gossip about how I was acting, because it would put my secret cure for Oscar on their radar screen. Evidently, I was already on probation.

"You naughty, naughty girl," Madame Torres's voice dropped and a smile crossed her bright red lips, exposing her snow-white teeth when she read my thoughts about asking for Aunt Helena's help. After all, Aunt Helena would surely help me find a way to cure Oscar Park without skipping a beat. "I love it."

The twins stopped shy of the door. Nonchalantly, I made my way to the front of the store and gently invited the two of them back in.

"Where are my manners? What can I do for you two lovely ladies this morning?" I took two bottles of hand cream and handed them to the sisters. "On me."

They snatched up the freebies as if they were a dead body.

"We have a little issue with Patience and the meeting tonight." Constance reminded me of my first meeting as Village President, and how Patience's future in the community was on the line.

"We can discuss it at the meeting." I patted her shoulder.

"But you are one of us, and you understand what it is like when things go awry." She tapped her nose. My brows furrowed. "Don't pretend you don't. After all of those years you lived as a mortal?"

"Yes." I took them by the arms and lead them back to the door. If I knew they wanted to talk about the charge against Patience of stealing animals from Petunia – which was on the agenda tonight – I would not have stopped them. "If you have forgotten, this is a place of business where our customers can *feel* the magic, but they don't really know that we are the ones *making* the magic. Let's keep it that way." I opened the door and held it wide. "Now, I will see you two tonight."

"Well." Constance puffed. "I never."

"Me either." Patience huffed right behind Constance.

"Be sure to only use a little dab of that cream on each hand." I could just see Patience covering herself in lotion from head to toe. "A dab will do you."

Right before I shut the door behind them, Mr. Prince Charming darted right back in.

"Look mommy, a kitty!" A cute little girl with freckles across her nose ran across the store after Mr. Prince

Charming, snagging the hem of one of the tablecloths and dragging it along with her.

Crash! The tablecloth fell, sending the bottles tumbling, leaving them broken all over the floor.

"I'm so sorry," the mother apologized before grabbing her daughter and rushing to the door, only to run smack dab into Ophelia Biblio. "Excuse us."

Ophelia smiled. "No problem," She said in a soft-spoken voice. She tilted her head, her eyes flickered with gold specks...*mesmerizing.*

"Mommy, I was only trying to catch the pretty kitty." The little girl grabbed her mom's face with both hands.

"It's okay!" I hollered after them, hoping they would come back in. "Geez." I shook my head looking at the mess. Ophelia walked over and stood next to the mess. I held a finger up. "I'll be right back."

"I'll be right out!" I yelled to Ophelia on my way to the storage room to grab an empty box to put all the broken pieces in. I didn't want her to leave. I wanted the "scoop" on Ever After Books and to ask what types of books she was carrying. Plus, I wanted to welcome her to Whispering Falls. After all, it was my presidential duty to be nosy about the new citizen.

The storage room was more like a little den that had a refrigerator and couch for those potion-making late nights. Unfortunately, I was pretty good at keeping things organized and didn't have an empty box.

"Maybe I have one out here." I walked out of the storage room and back into the shop, looking behind the counter just in case I had one there. No such luck. I turned my attention to Ophelia. "I guess I will have to..."

My mouth dropped. The mess had been cleaned up and everything was perfect, like the little girl was never there.

Ophelia tugged at the wrinkle in the red cloth, taking the crease right out.

She brushed her hands together. "There you go." She placed her hands in the front pockets of her jeans, and then rocked back on her wedge heels.

"Th…" I gulped. "Thanks."

In the year I had been in Whispering Falls, I had never seen anyone clean up so fast, say nothing about putting it back exactly the way it was before.

Slowly I walked around the small table, checking out the bottles that I swore were broken all over the floor.

A faint glow coming from the counter caught my eye. My cauldron was bubbling, almost boiling over with the potion I had made for Oscar before Mary Ellen sent it crashing to the ground earlier.

"How did you do that?" I clamped my hand over my mouth and fixed my eyes on Ophelia Biblio, waiting for an explanation.

"I'm Ophelia Biblio." Ophelia spoke with a soft, gentle tone that had a treble pitch. She stuck her hand out. I couldn't help but notice the ring on her right ring finger.

"You like charms." She dangled her finger. The small gold ring band had a small book charm hanging off of it.

"How did you know?" I asked. My intuition told me she had a kind soul.

She reached out and wrapped her fingers around my wrist. "You are wearing a charm bracelet, plus your cat has a charm dangling from his mouth."

Chapter Four

"He has what?" My stomach knotted before I even
looked Mr. Prince Charming's way. When he brought me a charm, it was a sure sign that
something good or bad, usually bad, was going to happen.
I gulped and slowly turned to Mr. Prince Charming.
There he sat as if he didn't have a care in the world as he
dragged his long white tail along the counter. Just as
Ophelia had said, there was something silver sticking out of
his mouth.

Meow, meow. His cry was more pathetic than normal
causing him to drop the charm in between his front legs. He
picked up his paw and licked it off before he raked it over
his ear.

"About that..." The shop door flew open and Bellatrix
Van Lou, Bella for short, stood at the door. She pointed
toward Mr. Prince Charming but withdrew once she cast
her eyes on Ophelia.

Bella smiled, exposing the gap between her two front
teeth. Her checks puffed out with a crimson touch. She
shook her head, her blond hair floated around her face,
casting a shadow around her smoky eyes.

"How rude am I?" Bella swept across the floor with
her hand extended. She looked up at Ophelia. Bella was
considerably shorter, standing at five-foot two-inches. Even
in her laced-up pointy red shoes, she was still short. With
style and ease, Ophelia took Bella's hand. "I'm so sorry. I
had no idea we were in the presence of a new spiritualist."

"Ophelia Biblio." Ophelia nodded. "You are the
astrologer in the community and owner of..." She tapped
her long skinny finger on her temple. The book charm
swayed back and forth from her ring with each tap.

"...Bella's Baubles." Her eyes lit up with a sparkle as pride showed on her face.

"Yes. How did you know?" Bella tilted her head. There was intrigue on her face and her eyes narrowed as if she were trying to figure out who Ophelia was.

"I'm the owner of the new bookstore across the street." Ophelia moved her finger from her temple and pointed toward the window.

Bella's and my eyes followed the line of Ophelia's arm, hand, and finger and looked across the street where the construction crew was no longer anywhere to be seen. There was only a line of people forming out the door of Ever After Books.

"That was fast." I gawked over Ophelia's shoulder. "There was just a crew there."

"What can I say? They work fast." Ophelia's brow lifted. "I guess I must go. Talk to you soon." Ophelia turned on the balls of her feet and pranced out the door.

"I...I..." For a moment, Bella and I stood there with our mouths open, unable to put into words how Ophelia had affected us.

There was something mysterious, yet comforting about her presence that was unexplainable.

Purr, purr, Mrrow. Mr. Prince Charming brought our attention back to the charm he had dropped on the counter.

Ahem. I cleared my throat. "I guess you may know something about that." I nodded toward the charm, almost afraid to pick it up.

Ding, ding. The bell over the door jingled when a handful of customers walked through the door.

"That is exactly why I came by." She took me by the arm and walked me back to the counter, away from the customers. "I'm a little on edge with the charm he choose."

Neither of us picked up the feather charm, but we both stared at it, both afraid to pick it up as though it was going to make us disappear or something worse.

"I love all my charms. I really do." I picked up Mr. Prince Charming and held him close. "But every time you give me one, it means that my life is about to get very complicated."

Rowl. He jumped out of my arms and darted underneath the table that had crashed and burned only a short while ago, only to be quickly put back together.

Nervously, I chuckled and picked up the charm. My intuition told me the angel wing charm might have something to do with Ever After Books.

"Tell me," I said, holding the charm to the light so I could get a better look. It wasn't any different than the charms I had seen the Hollywood stars wearing around their necks in the gossip magazines that lined the counter at the Piggly Wiggly in Locust Grove. "What is the meaning behind this chosen charm?"

Bella reached over and unclasped the bracelet from my wrist and held her hand out for me to drop the charm into her open palm. "Really, there isn't a bad meaning, just another protection. The meaning is sent from above, offering you guidance." Her voice trailed off.

I looked over at the picture hanging on the wall. Aunt Helena had given me a picture of Darla, my dad, and me from when I was a little girl, and I couldn't help but think that Darla had a hand in Mr. Prince Charming picking out this charm.

"Then it's about me being the new Village President." I protested, and ignored my gut, which would probably come back and bite me in the butt. That was what generally happened when I ignored my intuitive gifts. "And Darla had something to do with it."

"Mm…Hmmm," Bella agreed, but didn't sound all that convinced. "I guess we aren't going to discuss Ms. Biblio?"

"I'm not sure what to say," I leaned in and whispered. A couple of the customers were browsing the love potions that were sitting on the shelf along the wall. "I didn't catch what type of spiritualist she is, but I have a feeling it's a good one."

"You go find out and let me know when I drop off the bracelet, after I put the charm on." Bella waved over her shoulder on her way out.

"I can't quite put my finger on it," I mumbled, referring to Whispering Falls' newest villager, and I tapped Madame Torres. For a moment, we stared at each other and then averted our gaze to the window. "Find out everything there is to know about Ophelia Biblio."

Madame Torres's bright red lips curled into a smile, slanting her heavily glittered eyes.

"My pleasure." Her voice was low and sultry. The ball went black.

Chapter Five

"Good morning." I turned around to greet a few of the customers as I set samples of a new dry hand cream on the small silver trays on a couple of pedestal stands that were scattered throughout the shop.

Customers loved to try samples, which generally turned into a sale.

"These are hand cream samples." I extended a small tube to a woman checking out the homeopathic body scrubs. I didn't have to use my intuition to know she was looking to purchase something for her dry scaly hands. "May I?"

I held the sample out and gently took her hand in mine. *Sniff sniff.* The smell of roses, fresh cut grass, wood chips, and mulch filled my senses.

"I'm June Heal, the owner of A Charming Cure." Gently I rubbed the cream all over her hands and in between her fingers. The more I rubbed in the cream, the more my intuition told me she was an avid gardener. When someone needs a specific cure, my intuition always kicks in by letting me know exactly what ingredients to use, or what to add to something that was already available in the shop.

"I'm Mandy." She smiled and watched me rub her hand. "I have never found a good cream for my achy hands. My doctor told me that I was going to have to stop gardening because of the rash I get when I work in the garden, but I have fond memories of my mom and me working in the garden as a small child. And..." Tears swelled in her eyes.

"Let me see if I can help you." I patted her hand. She didn't need to tell me her mom had passed away and she was trying to hold on to everything they had. I could relate and physically feel her pain. "You look around and I will be right back."

A few other customers milled around the shop, but no one seemed to need my attention more than Mandy.

I made my way around the counter and disappeared behind the partition. It was the first time I was going to use my cauldron that Mary Ellen had broken into pieces and Ophelia Biblio zapped back together.

I flipped the switch on my black pot. It came to a rolling boil like it had never been broken. I ran my finger along the shelf to find the perfect ingredients to add to Mandy's very own cream.

The Indian hemp sparked when I touched it. I took it down from the shelf and uncorked it. There was just enough in there to enhance the cream and customize it to fit Mandy's needs...her memories.

"Hmm..." I rubbed Mr. Prince Charming as he walked around the bottles on the shelf. "I need one more thing." I tapped down the bottles to see exactly where I had put it. "Ah! I almost forgot that I hid you behind the vitamin B."

The Mojo Wish Bean glowed yellow. I held it to my heart. This wonderful bean was used specifically in special circumstances. It helped to manifest wishes and desires. A small dose will help bring back Mandy's fond memories of her mom.

I peeked around the petition to make sure the customers were okay and no one saw me take the Mojo Wish Bean down. If it got into the wrong hands, it could be disastrous.

"Boo!" Chandra Shango jumped out from behind the partition and threw her hands up in the air, nearly causing me to have a heart attack. Her yellow turban was cocked to one side. Her hazel eyes danced with delight. She cackled, pushing her raspberry-toned hair up into the jeweled turban.

"You scared me!" I held the Mojo Bean Wish bottle close to my heart.

"That was the idea." Her shoulders bounced up and down, trying to suppress a giggle. Her hands reached out and cradled my arms. With a squeeze, she chuckled, "I'm so sorry. I slipped in when you were talking to that customer about your hand cream."

"For some reason, I do not believe you are sorry." I winked and slipped the special ingredient into the front pocket of my apron. I was fond of Chandra. She was so full of life and so happy. "To what do I owe the pleasure this early morning?"

"My first manicure isn't for another half hour and I wanted to know what you thought about Ever After Books." Chandra fluttered her brows up and down. Glitter floated to the floor as it shook loose from the orange sparkly eye shadow heavily painted on her eyelids. "Alexelrod is all torn up about it."

I shrugged, playing coy and kept my hands busy. "There is nothing going on. Just a new business."

Chandra owned A Cleansing Spirit Spa right next door. She was the palm reader in our little magical village and I wanted to make sure she couldn't get a glimpse of my hands. Even though the Number One Rule in the spiritual handbook was that you cannot read another spiritualist without their permission, Chandra was known (a time or two) to read another villager without their permission.

We were all guilty of it...even me.

Chandra leaned up against the counter and watched as I continued to work on the special mixture for Mandy.

"Don't tell me that you are going to change now that you have been named the new Village President!" Chandra didn't seem to think the situation was so funny now.

"No, but I don't know anything about her or her business." The mixture was turning out nice and thick. "Ophelia seems to be nice."

Her heavy lashes flew up. "Ophelia? She just got into town and you already know her?"

"Ahhh…" I muttered. Being Village President and staying neutral was definitely going to be a challenge for me. "She came into the shop this morning and introduced herself, but I had a roomful of customers. I didn't get to ask her anything about the bookstore." I rubbed my hand on the cauldron that Ophelia had mysteriously put back together.

"Speaking of customers, I've got to go." Chandra tapped her watch and rushed through the shop, almost knocking that same table over…again.

"Mandy," I walked over and touched her on the forearm. "I'll be right back."

Mandy nodded. Her lips pursed in a simple, grateful smile.

The cauldron bubbled. I took a pinch of Indian hemp and threw it in. Using the ladle, slowly I stirred the white potion until it turned amber in color. The smell of flowers, grass, and mulch swirled above the cauldron, filling the air with the sweet smells of spring.

The murky substance glowed green. I took the Mojo Wish Bean bottle out of my apron pocket and uncorked the top. Tapping the bottle on my palm, one small teal bean popped out of the tiny hole. I threw the bean in and put the cork back on the bottle.

I put the bottle back where I found it and made sure to cover it up, out of sight.

The cauldron stopped boiling.

I held my hands over the liquid that had turned blue. With my eyes closed, I visualized Mandy working in the garden, and whispered, "Quiet mind, quiet soul, bring on the good memories the garden holds. Keep hands clean, keep them safe, and bring back the good memories in this place."

The liquid suddenly hardened. Slowly I stirred it to create a creamy lotion-like substance.

A bottle glowed from the shelf of empty potion bottles that was underneath the potion shelf. The bottles spoke to me by glowing when they wanted to be used. They were just as important to the cure as the cure itself.

I took the red heart-shaped bottle off the shelf. It was perfect for the wonderful memories that were going to be stored there. I held the bottle close to the cauldron and watched the magical substance fill the glass. I have never questioned how the magic worked.

A few minutes later, I had all the instructions on how to use the cream written on a piece of paper for Mandy to take home.

"It only takes a dab." I opened up the special bottle and put a dab on my finger. "No more than this." I took Mandy's hand and gently rubbed in the cream.

"It's like…" she gasped, "magic."

The one little dab was enough to cover both hands and more. She continued to rub her hands together. Her eyes twinkled with delight.

"Here are the instructions and how your hands will feel." I placed the instructions in the bag along with the bottle. I took her money. "When you need a refill, don't throw away the bottle. Bring it back and I'll be more than happy to fill it back up."

"Thank you so much." Mandy held the bag close to her and waved as she went out the door.

I walked over to the window to watch her leave, but there was some sort of commotion going on over at Ever After Books.

"Oh, no." I shook my head when I saw Alexelrod Primrose pacing back in forth in front of the bookshop with a picket sign.

Chapter Six

No sooner did I clear out the store, than Oscar Park walked in.

"What's going on?" He pointed to the sign I was flipping around and the customers that were walking out. "Aren't you open?"

"Oscar." My heart melted when I saw him. This was bad timing for a visit, but good timing for him to watch the shop. "You can do this." I grabbed him and pulled him into the shop. "Ladies," I called after the customers I had just kicked out. "My help is here, so we are staying open. Please come back in and take fifty-percent off any product of your choice."

The women happily agreed, but Oscar wasn't so thrilled about it.

"I..." He shook his head. "I don't know anything about these crazy homeopathic cures Darla taught you how to do. It wasn't so long ago that you set fire to your shed in Locust Grove."

Oscar reminded me of the unfortunate situation that happened before we moved to Whispering Falls; only he didn't remember the "we" part of it. I was working on a cure using the Magical Cures Book Darla had left me, only I didn't know it was an actual potion book and I blew up the shed. All of Locust Grove thought I was crazy. Shortly after that incident, I was happy to discover that I was a spiritualist and did belong to a community.

"You always worked with me at the flea market." I reminded him. "And Mr. Prince Charming is here."

I rushed over to the counter and grabbed Mr. Prince Charming. Neither of them had a great fondness for the other.

Grrrowl. Mr. Prince Charming wiggled out of my arms and batted at Oscar before he ran underneath one of the display tables.

"Yeah, sure, he wants me here." Oscar eyed the table.

"Yes he does!" I yelled over my shoulder. "I'll be right back."

I didn't bother looking behind me because I wasn't going to go back. Some tourists had already gathered around Alexelrod as he pumped the sign in the air and screamed, "Ever After Books will be the ever after of Whispering Falls!"

"I think he's lost his mind." Raven Mortimer nudged me when I walked up next to her. Her long black hair was pulled up into a high ponytail and swayed like a horse's tail when she shook her head. "He had to know the shop was coming to town. He *is* the only realtor after all."

She had a point. Why would Alexelrod suddenly protest Ever After Books, since he had to have sold the property to Ophelia?

His protest didn't stop the customers. They filed in one-by-one. I was sure they were there to see what all the fuss was about.

"Don't go in there," Alexelrod told the customers.

"Stop this." I tugged on the sleeve of his trench coat.

"No!" He glared at me. "If you aren't going to stop this, I will!" He pointed to himself.

I turned back around. The crowd had gotten larger. Izzy stood inches above the crowd in the back. She owned Mystic Lights, which disguised her gift of reading crystal balls.

Darting and dodging like a rat in a maze, I found my way to the back where she was standing.

She wore an A-framed skirt with light bulbs printed all over it and it hung past her knees right about where her boots started to lace down. Her hands were planted firmly on her hips with a scowl on her face.

"What am I supposed to do about this?" I asked.

"I don't know." She didn't bother taking her eyes off Alexelrod. "I do know that he has never acted this way before, which makes me believe he does have an issue with the store." She gathered her long blond hair in one hand and laid it over her shoulder.

"He showed up at my door very early this morning wanting to discuss the opening, but I told him it wasn't the time or the place and to leave it for the meeting tonight." Suddenly, I was regretting my decision not to listen to him. "What do I do about those situations and not let them lead to this?"

"You handle each situation as it arises. And this one *has* risen." She warned me right before Alexelrod's voice was heard screaming over the crowd.

"Whispering Falls will not have an ever after if this shop stays!"

"Great," I groaned and headed back to Alexelrod. There had to be something done to stop him. Ophelia seemed nice enough, although her powers excelled past mine and I didn't have a clue what her gift was, but I would find out soon enough.

"Head on over to The Gathering Grove and put on a strong pot of black coffee." I patted Gerald Regiula on the back when I made my way through the crowd. He caught his top hat that tumbled off when I startled him.

"Of course." His mustache bounced up and down as he agreed. He put the top hat back on and adjusted his yellow ascot. Gerald was always dressed to impress.

Petunia Shrubwood, Gerald's long-time "friend", stood next to him fiddling with a twig sticking out of her makeshift updo and had a chipmunk perched on top of her shoulder, which was a common sight with her since she was the owner of Glorybee Pet Store and animal physic.

"What can I do, June?" The corner of her hazel eyes dipped down in sadness. The chipmunk scurried away as she lost her footing and almost fell due to someone knocking into her to get a good look at the ranting Alexelrod.

"Oh, sorry!" Faith Mortimer pushed her newspaper-boy hat back up on her head, her long blond hair flowed from underneath it and her blue eyes lit up like the fireworks at our Halloween festival. "I'm getting the scoop!"

"She'd better get something to keep that paper alive." Officer Gandolf stood with his arms crossed. The city budget was another issue we were going to have to discuss at the village meeting. Unfortunately, the Gazette would be the first thing to go since subscribers were down.

I watched Officer Gandolf take his sweet time walking up to the front of the crowd as Faith darted in and out.

Faith was in charge of the one and only newspaper in our little community, *The Whispering Falls Gazette*. She was the sister of Raven Mortimer, but they sure did have different jobs and completely different personalities. Faith was a Good-Sider and Raven was a Dark-Sider, which was rare for spiritualist families, but stranger things had happened.

The Good-Sider Spiritualist, which was what I was, had an innate spirit to always do the good thing; to never do evil or harm to others. The Dark-Siders of the spiritual world had a tendency to be the wild children and did things to get themselves ahead of the game at anyone's expense.

Luckily, Raven was not that type of Dark-Sider. She was influenced by being raised in a Good-Sider family.

Until recently, Whispering Falls only accepted residents that were Good-Sider Spiritualists. Right before Izzy stepped down as Village President, the community voted to accept all spiritualists, including Dark-Siders. Since I was new, I was still discovering new spiritualists and their gifts. According to the Elders, I was the chosen one to lead.

"Watch where you are going next time!" Petunia scowled and before I could ask her to do anything, she stomped off in a rage toward Glorybee, the complete opposite of where I needed to be.

Faith threw her hand up in the air, which was her way of acknowledging Petunia's snide remark, but kept going. There was a story to tell and Faith was going to tell it.

It was a wonder that Faith didn't already know about Alexelrod. She was a Foreseer and was able to feel the community as a whole and report the news of any upcoming events, upheavals, or situations before anyone else could see or feel them. Most of the time Faith's predictions were vague, but she knew something was about to happen. The Whispering Falls Gazette was audio, which meant that if you were a subscriber your newspaper was delivered through the air via Faith's vocal chords in the morning. I didn't hear it this morning, but I also was disturbed by one Alexelrod Primrose.

I glared at him. He knew better than to act this way. He pranced back and forth, jabbing the sign up and down, marching in front of the bookstore's door so no one could go in.

"June." He continued to protest without even stopping to talk to me.

"What are you doing?" I asked in a "what in the hell are you doing" kind of voice.

"I told you. I'm going to do whatever it takes to get this bookstore out of Whispering Falls." His gaze left me and turned to Ophelia Biblio. She stood in the bookstore display window among the display of books, glaring at him. "We don't want you here!"

Ophelia was at her wits' end. The bookshop door flew open. A gust of wind rushed out, leaving us with wind-blown hair. In an instant, she stood on the step near the shop gate and used the wooden broom in her hand to push the gate open.

Ever so elegantly, Ophelia stepped out of the gate and pointed the broom handle toward Alexelrod.

Her voice held no room for discussion, "Mr. Primrose, kindly step away from my store, or you will meet your demise."

The crowd gasped as they saw the fury conveyed deep within her eyes.

It wasn't so much the anger she had deep within her that caught me off guard, which was probably acceptable to me since the protest was not substantiated, but it was her entire appearance.

Ophelia was not dressed in the jeans and shirt she had on earlier. The black button-up blouse was neatly tucked into a long black skirt, the hem hitting right at her ankles and black boots. But the hat; the hat was a dead giveaway. It had a wide brim with a pointy cone on top.

"Witch?" I whispered, hoping no one would hear me, bringing my hand up to my mouth.

Ophelia Biblio's lips turned up in a grin; her eyes lowered and her lashes cast a shadow on her fiery red cheeks. "Yes, I'm a witch."

Chapter Seven

A few minutes later, I had wrangled Alexelrod next door and into The Gathering Grove Tea Shoppe before Ophelia could turn him into a toad. Faith Mortimer was more than willing to help out for the low price of the scoop.

"As soon as you let me go, I'm going to march right back over there and protest." Alexelrod jerked away and flung himself in a chair at the café table nearest the window. He didn't take his eyes off the street. "If I'd have known who she was, I would have never let her move the bookshop into this village!" He banged his fist on the table.

"Calm down." I signaled Gerald to bring the coffee right away...for me.

Gerald set two different cups on the table, one filled with coffee and the other filled with tea and leaves. Suspiciously, I eyed Gerald, knowing exactly what he was up to with the leaves. He was trying to be sneaky. I ignored his tactics because I liked it.

Gerald's shop was his cover for his spiritual gift of tealeaf reading. After someone drank a cup of his specialty tea, the leaves left on the bottom and sides of the cup formed pictures, images that told the future of the recipient.

I picked a plastic stir stick out of the container in the middle of the table that was among the sugar and spices, and slowly stirred the coffee in my cup. I didn't want to have any unused coffee grounds for Gerald to read, not that I thought coffee grounds could be read, but I wasn't willing to risk the chance.

I had enough problems that needed to be kept to myself and not shared with the entire community.

I scooted the old smooth white Dalton cup toward Alexelrod. A long time ago, Gerald had told me how he used that particular teacup because it was smooth on the

inside, without any lips or curves, making it the best choice
for readings.

Gerald picked up the plain teapot with the open spout.
He said that it created the perfect flow for the leaves to be
poured out into the cup.

"Here you go..." Gerald poured the tea in the cup that I
had scooted in front of Alexelrod. "a bit of tea to calm your
nerves."

Alexelrod didn't even look at the cup before he picked
it up to take his first sip.

Shoo. Relief settled in my gut as I watched Alexelrod
drink the tea without question. Most spiritualists knew
when they were getting read by other spiritualists, but
Alexelrod's mind was definitely consumed with Ophelia
Biblio and Ever After Books.

"I understand you are very upset about the bookshop
opening today." Alexelrod needed a little empathy and I
was just the one to give it to him. I pushed the small cream
pitcher toward him. I wanted to make sure Gerald got a
good reading, even if I knew it was illegal to read
Alexelrod's leaves. The cream would make the leaves stick
to the cup better. "Whatever the issues are, we will discuss
them at the council meeting tonight. Isn't that right
Gerald?"

He winked, going along with my plan. "Let me get
more tea." Gerald rushed to the back of the shop and
behind the counter. There was a lot of clinking going on
back there as he worked diligently to get all the reading
material that we needed together for a good reading.

"It might be too late." Alexelrod picked up the teacup
and continued to stare out the window as he took small
sips.

"She just moved in." Gerald walked back. He poured
the steaming liquid into the cup when Alexelrod sat it back

in the saucer. Several leaves poured out, disappearing to the bottom. Alexelrod haphazardly stirred as Gerald poured. "It's not going to be too late."

The three of us sat in silence and watched Alexelrod polish off the tea. Faith sat at a distant table writing away in her reporter's journal, taking it all in.

This would definitely be front-page news in tomorrow's paper. By morning, I hoped there would be an explanation for his behavior.

"That was good tea," Alexelrod said and wiped his lips with the sleeve of his overcoat.

"Old chap, do you mind flipping the cup over in the saucer. I'm the only one working today and trying to keep things cleaned up." What Gerald had asked Alexelrod to do didn't make any sense. "If you flip over the cup for me, I can carry it back to the kitchen easier."

Alexelrod flipped over the cup without question, scooted back his chair, and stood up. Gerald and I eagerly watched him, waiting to hear what he was going to say, but more importantly what his tea leaves revealed. Faith put her pencil down.

None of us said a word. The air was thick with anticipation.

"I'm going to go take a nap." Alexelrod tapped the top of his cup three times. Gerald smiled, his mustache curling up on the edges, because Alexelrod was making his tealeaf reading more clear by tapping the upside down china. He placed his round-brimmed hat on his head, and facing forward he walked to the door. He held it open for a group of customers coming in before he walked out.

"Sit anywhere," Gerald said, but didn't pay any real attention to them.

We planted our faces up against the shop window to watch Alexelrod walk down the street. I had to make sure he wasn't going to go back to the picket line, but he didn't. He walked in completely the opposite direction.

Good thing he did. Ophelia must have called Officer Gandolf. He was standing in front of Ever After Books as if he were keeping guard. Something else I was positive I was going to get an ear full about.

"Well?" I turned around and looked at Gerald. What was he waiting for? We had tea leaves to read.

Gerald, Faith, and I nearly knocked each other over as we scattered to the café table to see the cup.

Ahem. Gerald cleared his throat. "Hold on." Gerald inhaled deeply with his eyes closed. A bit of relief settled in my tummy. There had to be a reasonable explanation for Alexelrod's behavior and the cup would tell the tale. "I had to make sure he was calm and didn't go back into the bookstore before I could read his leaves. If he had gone back into protest mode, the tea didn't have the calming effect, but as you see, it did."

"And?" Faith nodded toward the cup, suggesting Gerald stop explaining and do a little reading. Her pen was pressed up against her pad of paper ready to write down his reading.

Gerald flipped the cup back over to rest on the saucer. "The only thing he didn't do was turn the saucer around for us, which is how we call on the spirit of the cup to aid in the reading." He shook his head. "I really don't think that will be an issue though."

The tips of Gerald's fingers gingerly picked the cup up from the lip. Faith and I didn't move as Gerald went into explaining what he was doing.

"We will read from the handle down." He held the cup toward us. It looked like a bunch of mushy tobacco in the bottom and all over the sides. Nothing that I'd consider life-telling. "The handle represents his circle, which could be friends, home, and family." He ran his finger clockwise along the top of the teacup away from the handle. "These leaves will tell us what has happened in his life and things that are currently going away from him at this point."

Gerald stopped for a moment, dipping his head down closer to the cup. His eyes clouded over as sheer black fright crept across his face.

"Here," he pointed to the opposite side of the handle, "represents people that are not close family or friends, and he may not even know them."

For a moment, I zeroed in on the cup, taking a good look at the opposite end of the handle. My gut told me there was something that I should be seeing. I squinted trying to find a picture like one of those 3-D puzzles where you have to squint and stare for a period, taking your eyes out of focus until the picture was visible.

Nothing.

"This side of the cup," Gerald rounded his finger from the bottom lip of the cup to the other side of the handle, "is his future or things coming toward him." He shivered. His voice was bold, harsh. "I see nothing. Time to go, I have customers to serve."

"But there has to be something." I watched him gather the cup and saucer before he stood up. His hands were shaking. I pointed. "You see something and you aren't telling us."

Ahem. Gerald cleared his throat again, rushed behind the counter and disappeared into the back.

My cell vibrated in my back pocket, signaling me that I had a text.

Oscar: *when r u coming back*
Me: *soon*
Oscar: *hurry I do not know what I am doing*

"That was a waste of time when I could have interviewed him." Faith flipped her pad shut and stuffed her things into her messenger bag before she dashed out the door.

I waited a few minutes to see if Gerald was going to resurface, but he didn't so I left. I didn't have time to wait around any longer. I slipped out of the teashop and noticed the crowd that was once gathered to watch Alexelrod had dissipated. The bookstore was packed, confirming that Alexelrod had brought even more attention to the shop, and everyone wanted to go in to see what all the fuss was about.

"Hmm…" Briefly, I stopped and looked in. Ophelia was helping a customer in the aisle marked "Travel" and they chatted away. "She can't be all that bad," I murmured and hurried on my way.

I had never come across a true witch before and wasn't sure what to think of it. I had to get back to the shop to make sure Oscar was okay, but more importantly, what Madame Torres had found out about our new spiritualist.

Chapter Eight

"Eloise." I was surprised to see A Charming Cure filled with customers and Eloise Sandlewood helping Oscar out behind the counter. "What are you doing here?"

I tried not to let on that it was not a good idea for her to be helping Oscar. She was his aunt from his father's side of the family and the cleansing spiritualist of the community.

Eloise's emerald eyes were glittering with delight as she spoke, "I came to see you and found this nice young man in your place." She stood behind Oscar and put each of her hands on his biceps. She closed her eyes and took a deep inhale.

"I couldn't have done it without you." Oscar stepped away causing Eloise to drop her hands. "It's my day off, so I have to get back home and cut the grass."

"Oh, okay." I forced a smile, even though sadness filled my soul.

I wanted so badly to tell him about the new shop and how Ophelia was a witch, not to mention Alexelrod's strange behavior. Oscar would have loved to figure that mystery out…if only he were still a spiritualist.

"Hey," He touched my forearm. "Are you okay?"

I waved my hand in the air, brushing him off. "Yea, I'm just super busy that's all." I nodded toward all the customers that had formed a line to check out.

"Why don't I bring by some Chinese tonight?"

"Great!" There wasn't a moment I didn't want to spend with him, and Chinese was our favorite.

"No." Eloise scowled. She lifted her brows. "You are busy. Remember?"

"Oh! Yea, right." I had completely forgotten about the council meeting. It was definitely one I couldn't reschedule. There was a bit of regret in my heart that I had accepted the role of Village President. "I have…"

There really wasn't a good excuse that I could think of.

"Girl's night." Eloise tugged at the ends of her short red hair, and then pulled her long black cloak around her. Even though she put a smile on her face, I could tell she wanted to hug Oscar and tell him that she was his aunt and he was a spiritualist at heart.

I snapped my fingers. "Yes. I planned a girl's night. What about tomorrow night?"

"I don't get off work until seven."

"Then eight will do." I smiled.

"I'll be at your new house at eight with a couple sacks of food." He walked over to the door and kept his hand on the handle. "I'll get something for you too, Mr. Prince Charming." He winked and rushed out.

Hiss, hiss. Mr. Prince Charming was good at showing his distaste for all things Oscar.

Eloise and I worked side-by-side until all the waiting customers were taken care of. Thankfully, I didn't have to make any special potions for any of them.

"I'm glad you are here, but you can't be talking to Oscar about anything magical." I warned her as I replenished the shelves.

"He still doesn't remember anything from the past year. Not even me," Eloise said with sadness.

I shook my head slowly. "I wish." I recalled the last time he did remember he was a spiritualist.

We had spent some time together under the stars near my cottage. The fireflies were out playing tag. It was almost like our very own fireworks show. He told me he loved me and sealed it with a kiss. I felt like I had floated to the moon and back on a comfy cloud. I couldn't wait until the next day to see him, but by then it was too late. He had gone to the Order of Elders without telling me, denouncing his spiritualist heritage in order to help me.

"I came in to ask you about the new bookshop." Eloise brought me back from my thoughts.

"Not you too." I turned all the bottles on the antacid homeopathic cures shelf so the labels were facing out. "I don't think I can take much more of this."

"What?" She drew back. "I think it's a great shop. I want to start a book club. How much fun would that be?"

"A book club?" The idea did sound like a lot of fun. Now that I was single, I could probably carve out an extra night in the month to go and hang out with my friends. "I love the idea."

"Good." Eloise slipped off the apron and hung it back on the hook on the wall. "I'm going to go and get ready for the meeting. I'm sure you need to prepare. And I'll let you know about the book club."

Eloise hugged me exactly the way Darla would have. I was lucky to have Eloise in my life. Not only was she special because she was part of Oscar, but she and Darla had been best friends.

Darla wasn't a spiritualist and I was too young to know if I had any spiritual gifts, so Darla and I moved to Locust Grove, right next door to Oscar.

"I can't wait to hear about it." I squeezed her back, missing Darla with each passing second. "Now," I pushed away, "I have to get ready for the meeting."

The clock on the wall let me know it was closing time. I had no idea what I needed to do for the meeting except show up.

Chapter Nine

Closed. I flipped the sign on the door. It started out as
a long day with Alexelrod showing up first thing and it was
going to be a long night with the meeting. I was sure the
hinges on the door at A Charming Cure were going to fall
off with all the customers coming in and out. There was no
way I was complaining about the business. It was much
welcomed, and I was happy that Alexelrod's little stunt
didn't hurt business.

Meow, meow. Mr. Prince Charming jumped off one of
the tables and circled my ankles in his signature figure-
eight style.

"Thanks." I bent down and cradled him in my arms.
Loving on him always calmed my nerves. His intuition was
just as spot on as mine. He knew when I was nervous and
tried to help me through it. That was one of the many
things I loved about Mr. Prince Charming being my fairy
god-cat.

"I'd be nervous too." Madame Torres, my snarky
crystal ball, glowed from the counter. Her flaming, curly
red hair tumbled all over, framing her bright red lips and
painted blue eyes. "It isn't every day you get to hold your
first village council meeting as the new president. I can't
wait to see Patience Karima's face when you put her in the
slammer!"

"Now stop it," I said as I opened the Magical Cures
Book. I was nervous. It was my first meeting and
Patience's theft of the ostrich was first on the agenda. Only
I wasn't convinced it was theft.

Recently, there had been an unusual amount of animals
showing up in our small village of Whispering Falls.
Everyone assumed Petunia Shrubwood would take care of
them since she was the owner of Glorybee Pet Store and

the local animal spiritualist. She could speak to animals, so we naturally assumed she'd take care of the new animals in town.

When an ostrich was reported missing, I dug around through a little investigating on my own. I found the darn bird in the embalming room right next to Patience as she hummed away while working on a body at Two Sisters and A Funeral Home. It was the one and only funeral home in the village, and Patience and her sister Constance owned and lived there.

The beady-eyed bird was just as odd as Patience herself, making them a good match for each other.

"I guess we will see what the council says." I fiddled around the tables to make sure everything was restocked and ready for tomorrow morning. There was nothing worse than coming to work and having to rush around to get things ready for customers – which I've had to do on a handful of times, because I had been too lazy to do it the night before.

Not tonight. I had to use my time wisely and that meant spending time around the cauldron.

"I have a few more leads on Make-Me-A-Match." Madame Torres caught my attention.

"Interesting." I scratched my chin. "Ophelia is pretty and she does seem to be nice like her profile says. I wonder why she needs Make-Me-A-Match."

Madame Torres glowed hot pink and small red hearts floated in her globe as if someone had picked her up and shook her.

"Not for Ophelia," Madame Torres cautioned me. "Her profile says '**MATCHED**' in big bold red letters."

Matched? Did Ophelia have a man in her life? Was he here with her?

"Then for who?" A niggling suspicion told me she was holding something back.

"Don't get mad, but we think you need to find someone." Madame Torres paused before she spewed words out like a volcano. "I made you a profile on Make-Me-A-Match."

Swaying a bit, I leaned up against the counter. "You what?" I put my finger in my ear and wiggled it. I thought for sure she said something about me.

"Please don't make me say it again." Her voice was tight as she spoke. I could tell she was a little uneasy about saying what I thought she said...*again*.

"I don't think I heard you correctly." If I did hear what she said, then we'd have an entirely different situation on our hands. I put my hands on my chest. "I thought you said you signed *me* up for Make-Me-A-Match."

I laughed, knowing I had completely heard her wrong. After all, I had Oscar, even if he didn't remember it. That reminded me to get back to my potion, because he would remember when he drank my little concoction.

"I didn't use those words exactly, but something to that effect." Her lips turned down in a grimace.

"No you didn't!" I grabbed the ladle off the counter and jabbed it toward her.

Madame Torres's shoulders rose and her eyes squeezed shut. "You aren't going to shatter me with that are you?" Skulls floated in the globe around her head, and the funeral march chimed out of the base of her ball.

Gently, I lowered the ladle onto the counter, flipped on the cauldron switch and decided to take a few deep breaths.

"June, you have been so bummed and you need to go out and find someone like...like..." Her globe shined like the sun.

"Like Oscar?" I asked.

"No. Like you," she warned.

"I have Oscar," I reminded her.

"No you don't. He doesn't understand who you really are now."

"He will remember." I started to pluck different ingredients off of the shelf. Most of the items I wouldn't use, but I had to keep my hands busy or I'm afraid I would have picked up Madame Torres and smashed her against the wall.

"No he won't."

"Shut up!" I rushed over to her ball with my hands full of bottles and screamed. "He loves me! He told me!"

"He told you that when he was a spiritualist. He denounced his heritage for his entire life." Madame Torres's lines creased on her forehead as her brows dipped, causing her purple turban to tilt forward. I secretly wanted it to cover her nose and mouth so she couldn't breathe.

Heat rose in my throat. I felt like I was going to be sick.

"June, are you okay?"

I shook my head, clearing my thoughts. A loud knock echoed and the door flew open.

"Don't you have a meeting to get to?" Raven Mortimer stood in the door way with a plateful of June's Gems. I put the bottles on the counter and rushed over to grab one of the delicious treats that she named after me. "I thought you might need a stress relief before the meeting."

I stuffed it in my mouth. All I could do was chew and nod.

"I didn't realize how stressed you really were…" She moved across the floor and put the rest of them on the counter. Mr. Prince Charming jumped up to get a good scratch from her. Raven had the best nails in town. "Until I was baking my new batch of Gems and I saw a few things that might be of interest to you."

That got my attention. I swung my head around, gulped, and licked my lips. Nervously, I asked, "What did you see?"

I wasn't really sure if I wanted to know, but Raven could tell a lot of things without being caught by Rule Number One. She was a Dark-Sider who practices Aleuromancy. Forms appeared in the baking dough she used. Most of the time she would see a form and just the right customer would come in for that exact baked good or pastry, and with her fantastic spiritualist skills, she was able to know it was for them.

"I wasn't sure until now that these were for you." She smiled, folding her hands in front of her as though she knew I was going to devour another one. She was right. I grabbed another June's Gem but took two bites instead of one this time.

She pointed to the door. "You really should lock your door when you are closed." Her features hardened. "You never know what can happen around here."

I walked over to lock the door so no one else would disturb me, but Ophelia Biblio caught my attention. She was putting a glass box on the steps of Ever After with a chalkboard sign that read: *Free Library. Take One, Leave One.*

That's a good idea, I thought.

Raven came over to see what I was looking at. "I had some doughnuts come up with the book forms in them." Her voiced drifted off to a distant place.

"What?" I asked. It wasn't my intuition that caught me off guard, it was Raven's odd behavior. She saw a book. Big deal.

"It wasn't just a book." Her eyes made contact with mine. There was a red ring around her pupil. "There were some sort of daggers or arrows stuck in them." She bit her lip.

When I looked at her a little longer, Raven was not with me. There was a faraway look deep in her eyes as though she was seeing the image again.

Her words and her actions made my stomach drop down to my toes. Instantly I thought of Alexelrod, but knew he would never hurt Ophelia.

"What does that image mean?" I asked, but there was no response, like she didn't even hear me. She sat straight as a stick with her hands neatly placed in her lap. "Raven?"

Her body shook, bringing her back from wherever she was.

"I'm sorry." She smiled. "I have no idea what just happened."

Raven picked around the items on the counter and didn't respond to any of my questions. She obviously didn't want to discuss what she had seen, just like Gerald. It was strange that both of them saw something very disturbing and neither of them wanted to discuss it.

"Oh!" Raven jumped out of her seat. "That reminds me. Your Gems were very specific today."

"In what way?" I eyed the free library, wondering if there were any potion books over there. Spell books were rare and hard to come by. That was why I had to see Aunt Helena at Hidden Hall A Spiritualist University and get the concoction for Oscar's cure. I had one shot and one shot only. I brushed my hands down my apron and went back to the cauldron. There wasn't any time to dilly dally with Raven when my heart was on the line.

My eyes zeroed in on Madame Torres. Anger was deeply rooted in my soul from her match-making skills that were not needed. I grabbed the bottle of bitter cucumber and threw it into the boiling cauldron.

"I have to think it was Darla trying to come through again." Raven picked up different bottles and looked at the labels before setting them back on the counter. "Some sort of broken heart with a rope around it trying to keep it together with a "D" printed on it. Maybe she needs to see you?"

If only, I thought as I stirred the pot before sticking in a small piece of Blue Darlwing. Once I had overheard that, the Blue Darlwing would bring back lost powers. On second thought...I reached over and grabbed another piece.

"I think it has to do with Oscar. I'm sure she is trying to tell me to move on just like the rest of my spiritual guides." I dismissed the forms because I wasn't ready to give up on Oscar just yet. Haven't they seen all of those articles that stated a person had to be ready to move on?

I was nowhere near ready.

"Could be." Raven threw her long black hair behind her shoulder before grabbing an apron off the hook. She took the bottle of Thistle Thorax off the shelf. "Here. I heard this helped with restoration."

She winked when I took the bottle. Without even having to tell her what I was going through, she understood.

It hadn't always been this way with Raven. We met at the University and had an immediate distaste for one another. Her Dark-Sider ways couldn't be trusted, and I was the Dean's niece who had a target on her back as the "new prodigy" in the spiritual world.

Strange events brought us together and we were fortunate to realize we were more alike than not. That was when she and Faith decided to move to Whispering Falls and set up a new life since we had just become an open spiritual community.

I glanced over at her. She still had the empty look in her eyes.

"Are you okay?" I asked.

She shrugged, and then walked over to see what I was doing.

The liquid in the cauldron twirled, creating a mini-tornado in the air. Sparks flew up and a display of fireworks filled the space above the swirling wind before the pot completely stopped.

"That was weird." Raven stood back. She had the ends of the apron covering her face as though she thought I was going to let something explode.

"Really? You think I'm going to blow up the place?" I asked and stirred the mix.

"Well…" she laughed, "with your history and all. But it's not every day I see a potion made." She did have me on that one.

"It's not every day a man would give up his entire future for me." My heart ached to think about what Oscar had done and that someone loved me that much. It was my duty to do everything in my power to reverse what the Elders had done to him.

"I'm sure you're right about the image, but I wanted to make sure that I told you and let you know what I saw." Her lips curled into a half smile. There was something telling me that she didn't buy into my reasoning, even though she said she did.

The potion needed a little breathing room, so I walked from behind the counter. The length of the meeting would give it just enough time to settle. By that time, I'd know if it worked or didn't.

Some chattering outside of the shop was getting louder and louder. It was almost time for the meeting. The cure was going to have to wait a little longer. Raven and I watched some of the villagers pass by A Charming Cure on their way to the Gathering Rock, which was a neutral and spiritual place where all the meetings convened. It was located on the hill between my cottage and the village.

Petunia was talking to someone outside of the shop. Her hand flew up in the air. It looked like a heated conversation between Petunia and Patience Karima.

Earlier, I had told both of them to steer clear of one another in fear they would argue and fight, and it looked like neither of them took my advice.

Petunia's face crinkled and she turned on the heels of her shoes, stomping off in the direction of the meeting. Patience crossed her arms over her housedress staring at Petunia as she walked away.

"If looks could kill," I murmured under my breath.

"What?" Raven asked from across the room.

"Tell me about the images you saw for Ophelia." I wanted to give Raven one more shot at telling me about the books and daggers. "I feel like something bad is going to happen and I can't put my finger on it."

I wanted my prying to be on the QT with casual conversation, so I milled around the shop gathering all the stuff I needed for the meeting, which included getting some items for a pre-meeting smudging ceremony together.

I figured I would do a quick smudge to create harmony since we had a lot of things on the docket that could create an uproar. Heading it off at the pass would bring the meeting to order and might bring some peace before the fallout.

Raven sat on the stool that butted up to the counter. She planted her elbows on the counter and rested her head in her hands. She talked while I gathered the smudging sticks and ingredients and put them in my bag.

"I'm not sure the images are for her, but there were several images of books that were ripped to shreds. Those daggers gave me the willies." She lifted her brows. "And it's not a coincidence that Ever After Books appeared right after I made the doughnuts."

"Hmm…" I grabbed a few Mojo Bags and stuck them into my satchel. If what Raven saw was true and it represented what was to come, I'd like to give one of the Mojos to Ophelia to keep her safe.

Mojo Bags were my little creation in a drawstring bag that customers could take home with them to create a sense of wellbeing. Some of them are custom-made, but a general one for Ophelia would be good until I got to know her.

"Did you know she is a witch?" I asked.

"A witch?" Raven gasped, lifting her head off her hands. "Has there ever been a witch in Whispering Falls?"

Raven hopped off the stool and followed me to the door.

"Not to my knowledge." I shook my head and flung the pack over my shoulder. It was time to go. There was a flurry of activity on the street from people rushing to the meeting and stopping to greet one another. "Now that we are an open community, I bet there will be all sorts of spiritualists coming in and out of this place."

The bowl of crystals on the table to the right of the door caught my intuition. Crystals were used for many things in the homeopathic world. I grabbed the bowl and dumped them into my bag. They would make a great gift to give out for the villagers who came to the meeting, not to mention, I could rub them with some cedar or sage before I gave it to them. That way they could put the crystal in their store or in their home with the purifying agent to help with any evil that tries to come into our community. And the way things were going, I didn't doubt that something was on the horizon.

I locked the door and pulled it shut.

"Lucky for us, you are in charge," Raven said as we made our way into the crowd and up the hill to a waiting community.

Yeah, lucky for us. There was a nagging doubt in my gut.

Chapter Ten

"Good evening," I greeted everyone with a smile and raised my arms to the sky. It was my way of letting everyone know that the meeting was about to begin and they could stop gossiping about Alexelrod Primrose's strange behavior.

The cloak that I had borrowed from Izzy was too long in the sleeves and torso, but it was going to have to do until I went shopping at Wands, Potions, and Beyond.

I reached into my bag, grabbed a couple of handfuls of crystals and stuck them in the pocket of the cloak.

Everyone stood around the Gathering Rock, forming a circle. They were shoulder to shoulder. I had never seen such a big crowd for a village meeting.

I laid the bundle of sage, sandalwood, cedar and Frankincense on the rock and lit it. I blew on the flame to create the smoke that was needed to fill the air around us.

Petunia Shrubwood stood next to Gerald with a scowl on her face, never once taking her eyes off of Patience.

Patience wrung her hands in front of her with her eyes closed as though she were praying.

I wasn't sure who she was praying too, but I sent up a little extra whisper because I was sure Petunia had created a very strong case against Patience and wanted full punishment, which would allow Patience to stay in the community, but strip her from ever performing her spiritual powers in Whispering Falls.

"Good evening, Petunia." I greeted her and pointed to her messy up-do with the eagle feather sticking out from the top of it. "Is that for me?"

She plucked it out of her hair and a little chipmunk scurried out and perched on her shoulder.

"I'm ready to get this over with and get rid of those animals." Petunia handed me the feather that she was so gracious to give me for every smudging ceremony from the bald eagle that lived at Glorybee.

With the bundle lit, I walked along the inside of the circle and fanned the smoldering bundle with the eagle feather. I started from the head and worked my way down to the feet on every single person who attended the meeting. After each personal smudge, I took a crystal out of my pocket and rubbed it on the bundle before handing to them. Then I took the sage side of the bundle and gave them a quick wave with the feather.

The sage would help drive away any bad spirits that might be trying to hurt our little community. I made sure to look in everyone's eyes to see if my intuition gave me anything, but it didn't. Not until I got to Ophelia.

"You can pass me up." She politely stepped back out of the circle and clicked her heels together. For a brief moment, our eyes met. I was determined not to blink or look-away, like the strategy I had when I was on the elementary school play yard in a mean game of stare-off. Ophelia didn't budge. The only reason I quit was because I had a meeting to hold.

Once around, I stood in front of the Gathering Rock and waited for some of the community leaders, Gerald, Izzy, and Chandra, to take their places on the bench-style seating so everyone could be comfortable.

"Where's Faith?" I mouthed to Raven. Faith was supposed to take notes and give a brief synopsis of the meeting in the morning paper.

Raven shrugged the old "I don't know." With or without her, I had to start the meeting.

The Marys floated on the outskirts of the meeting with their legs and arms crossed, taking everything in.

"Wow, this is a big crowd." I didn't want to be too formal. They knew me for who I was, not for someone I felt like I needed to be. "I would like to bring our first order of business to the forefront."

Petunia fidgeted in her spot while Patience whimpered into the handkerchief in her hand.

"Petunia Shrubwood, can you please come forward and state your claim?" It was very difficult to sound so professional when it was in my nature to make everyone happy. Including the always crabby Karima sisters.

Petunia stood up, running her hands along the front of her skirt. She tugged at the hem of her shirt, pulling it down before adjusting the sticks in her hair. She walked forward to the small podium. A white dove flew down and rested on her shoulder.

I couldn't help but wonder if it was a soul from the past. That was the thing with animals. When people died, their souls can sometimes came back in the form of an animal. A dove symbolizes love and peace, so I was sure that the soul that possessed the dove was a decent, caring soul who was looking out for Petunia.

"As you know," she opened her hands in a gentle way toward the meeting space to address the attendees. The wind whipped and the leaves in the trees rustled back and forth. Petunia didn't continue until the noise was clear, but that wasn't going to happen until all of the animals surrounding us had circled the Gathering Rock.

Deer, squirrels, birds, and even moose had formed their own little meeting on the outskirts of ours.

Ahem, Petunia cleared her throat. "As you know," she started again, "I am the spiritualist that can talk to animals. By the looks of things, they think I have something to tell them."

"Smiik, kiic, triic." Petunia threw her head back and made the worst sounding noise I had ever heard, causing the animals to scatter.

Everyone stared at the animals scurrying back to their homes in the woods that set just beyond the Gathering Rock. Again, we waited for the rusting leaves and hoof noises to stop before she continued.

"I'm sorry. I had to let them know it was a human meeting, not an animal one." Petunia's eyes sparkled as she talked about her gift, making me a little envious of her talent when all I could do was throw a few ingredients together. "A couple of months ago, several exotic animals showed up at Glorybee. None of them can talk to me so we can safely say they are not souls. Through endless searching with no luck, I have tried to find out where they have come from."

As she told the community her story, which we all already knew, I carefully watched the Karima sisters. Patience kept nudging Constance with her chubby elbow while Constance continually shushed her silently with her hands.

"Anyway, there is this crazy ostrich that doesn't like to be around the other animals." Petunia turned toward me and the other council members. Softly she spoke, "I thought the ostrich was stolen. But I was quite wrong. The ostrich does not like being at Glorybee but loves Two Sisters and A Funeral. Patience Karima takes good care of the ostrich and will take full responsibility until I find the rightful owners."

I slammed down the gavel before me. I had never used a gavel, but I have seen in many movies where the judge used one to make the audience come to order. Even though the meeting audience wasn't rowdy, I wanted to slam the gavel to make a motion to throw out the claim that Patience Karima had stolen the ostrich.

Bang, bang, bang. I secretly liked the feeling of the power behind that small hammer.

"You can stop the banging now." Gerald reached over and touched my arm. "You have everyone's attention."

"Oh." I giggled and stood back up. "Thank you Petunia for that bit of insight. We can move on to the next topic if that's okay."

Patience nodded her head so fast, I thought it was going to bounce right off her jolly shoulders. There was a smile planted across her face that puffed out her rosy cheeks.

"First, I'd like to officially welcome Ophelia Biblio to Whispering Falls." I pointed the gavel in her direction, but she was gone. "Ms. Biblio?" I shouted over the crowd that had now turned their backs on me and were looking around for her.

"It looks like she didn't hang around for the meeting." Izzy stood up. "I haven't seen her or Alexelrod Primrose for a while now."

"That's odd." Gerald cleared his throat. "I thought Alexelrod would be front and center after the little stunt he pulled today."

I glanced over at Gerald who didn't look up at me. I leaned his way and whispered, "What did his leaves say?"

"He's dead!" A woman's voice screamed from Main Street, echoing all the way up to the Gathering Rock. "Help! He's dead! Alexelrod Primrose is dead!"

Chapter Eleven

"Clear the way." Officer Gandolf ordered as he cleared a path on the steps of Ever After Books where Alexelrod Primrose was laying stone dead. This time Officer Gandolf wasn't as gentle as he yelled in his baritone voice, "Clear the way!"

Sirens blared as the Two Sisters and a Funeral hearse roared down Main Street. The crowd scattered like flies trying to get out of its way. Constance Karima didn't care who she ran over because it would be a score for her. Just another fresh body to bury and keep her in business.

"Out of the way! Fresh body!" Patience had her head stuck out the window shouting to the crowd, the ostrich's head stuck right out there beside hers.

The hearse came to a roaring stop. Constance jumped out and flung open the back door to retrieve the gurney.

Patience and the beady-eyed bird stood next to her. Patience repeated, "Umm hmm, fresh body!"

The gurney clicked once it hit the ground.

My heart sank when I realized that Alexelrod really was dead. Bella, Petunia, Faith, Raven, Izzy and I stood down the sidewalk with our heads bowed, not a word spoken between us.

"I can't believe I found him." Tears dripped down both sides of Faith's face.

My gut told me this was not an accident, but I wanted to believe otherwise until something was confirmed.

"Something isn't right around here." Chandra Shango walked up, dabbing her eyes with a tissue. "Do you think he is really dead?"

"By the looks of it, yes." Izzy nodded toward the bookstore. "He isn't moving."

"He was such a nice guy. Always so helpful when I was looking to open Wicked Good and needed a great space." Raven shook her head.

Sadness laid heavy on all of our hearts...all except for two. The Karima sisters, obviously.

"Coming through!" Constance barreled through the crowd in front of Ever After Books, slamming the gurney into the gate like a battering ram. The ostrich ran right behind. The gate flew. Patience didn't miss a beat when the gate flung back and hit her in the booty.

I rolled up on my toes to see above the crowd that had gathered to watch the spectacle, only to roll back down when my intuition told me that someone or something was watching me. My eyes gazed up the side of the building and stopped when I saw the curtain from the window on the second floor move slightly. Someone was looking down at the commotion and I couldn't help but think it was Ophelia, only I couldn't make out if it was or not.

The curtains closed when the person saw me looking up. My attention was then turned back to Ever After Books where Gandolf was talking to one very upset Faith Mortimer. Though this was out of my jurisdiction and had nothing to do with being Village President, I still made my way up to where the Karima sisters had already thrown a sheet over poor ole Alexelrod's body.

The ostrich pecked at the sheet with its beak. Patience tried to shoo him away, but he started pecking at her. It would have been a comical scene if Alexelrod wasn't lying there dead.

I still couldn't believe he was dead. My eyes filled with tears when I caught sight of his long black trench coat. He was a good man and a good realtor.

"Looks like we are going to have to figure out what killed him, sister." Constance Karima pulled back the white sheet. Her face scrunched up in scowl. "Look at that ear."

I tried to get a quick look, but Patience stepped in the way, causing my eye to venture down to her feet. She stood on the step leading up to the shop, right next to the flowerbed where Ophelia had neatly planted two berry bushes and some rainbow daisies. It wasn't the flowerbed or the daisies that caught my eye. It was the book that was lying under a bush. Its corner was barely visible to the naked eye.

"Is there anything I can do?" I walked between the Karima sisters and put my arms around both of them. I didn't want to mention that it was probably a heart attack from the stress of him trying to stop Ophelia from opening Ever After Books this morning.

Constance shrugged me off. "What is wrong with you June Heal? This here is a murder investigation, in case you can't tell."

"Murder?" I looked around to make sure no one was looking as I stuck my toe behind me and gently nudged the corner of the book a little further under the bush. "Aren't you taking this murder thing a little too far? We don't want to alarm the citizens that there may be a killer on the run."

I knew one should never assume someone was murdered and also not to freak out an entire community. Besides, Alexelrod was a good man. Who would want him dead?

The curtain in the window swung open, sending my eyes upward. There was no one there.

"Look here." She pulled back the sheet, and as sure as I was standing there, Alexelrod Primrose had indeed met his maker. She pointed to the swollen red marks just below his ear lobe on his neck. "It looks like he got a bug bite and

died. It could happen." Her brows lifted, and her neck skin
waddled as she nodded.

"Hmm..." I looked closer at the two spots. There was
no way that they could tell if that was an insect bite. "It
looks like zits to me." Not that I was making light of the
situation, but the Karima sisters had to be stopped from
speculating out loud.

The crowd was already whispering about a murderer
on the loose. I even heard the words serial killer from a few
audible whispers.

"Zits." Patience cackled, abruptly stopping when
Constance shot her *the* look.

"Grown men don't have acne." Constance lifted the
gurney and without warning, she rushed Alexelrod's body
to the hearse.

"Yes they do," I whispered under my breath. I had
several clients who had adult acne, but wasn't going to
discuss it further with Constance. Besides, she was already
knocking people out of the way with the gurney. I couldn't
help but feel sorry for Alexelrod. He wouldn't want the
village to see his lifeless body thumping and bumping
down the sidewalk.

Everyone was too busy watching the Karimas and their
circus act to see me reach down and pick the book up out of
the bushes. I wiped the dust off the front covers.

"Mysteries and Magical Spells," I sucked in air and
tucked the book up under the cloak I still had on from the
council meeting when someone called my name.

"What did you say?" Gandolf walked over and stood in
the spot where Alexelrod's dead body had been, sending
chills up my legs.

"I just can't believe it." I shook my head playing off
the little treasure lying just behind the cloak. "He was such
a nice man. I really can't believe he is gone."

"Well, if this is murder, we are going to have to keep it hush hush within our community." He cast down his eyes. "I'm going to have to expect nothing less than full cooperation from the council."

"Nothing less," I assured him. I shifted my body to my left side to help juggle the book in a comfortable position.

I tried to shoo the pesky ostrich away as he continued to jab his pointy bill at my feet.

Gandolf's curious eyes looked at the bird, and he muttered, "Crazy thing."

The bird popped his head up. There was something shiny sticking out of his mouth.

"What in the world?" Gandolf put his hand out. The bird dropped the object into Gandolf's hand. He held it up to the sunlight to get a better look.

Evidently that wasn't good enough. He pulled a small pair of reading sunglasses from the front pocket of his Whispering Falls uniform and put them on. He pulled the object closer to his eyes. Putting it to his nose, he took in a big whiff.

My heart stopped when I got a good look at it. "Is that a dart?" I tried to steady my shaking hands and voice.

The Karima sisters and I stood still; the crowd was silent. Everyone waited to see what Officer Gandolf had to say. The bird even stood still like he was a proud peacock.

"Yes! It's a poison dart and it's filled with poison!" He lifted the dart in the air for the gathered crowd to see. A collective gasp ripped through the crowd.

Constance Karima whipped out a clear baggie with the word *evidence* written in big black bold letters across it. This was right up her alley.

"Are you sure?" I tapped Gandolf's forearm. There was no reason to alarm anyone if it wasn't truly murder.

The ostrich pranced back and forth. It's head jabbed into the bushes coming back up with another dart.

"Positive," Gandolf confirmed when the bird gave him the second dart. "Two holes. Two darts. And blood." He pointed to a little spackle of blood on the sidewalk.

"So much for keeping it under wraps," I murmured under my breath.

The crowd was no longer in a hushed whisper. They were more like a gang of gaggling geese, all taking at once.

Patience Karima took the yellow crime tape and not only draped it across the Ever After Books front door, but looped it around every inch of the outside of the shop. Ever After Books was now a full-on crime scene.

Chapter Twelve

On my way into the shop the next morning, I couldn't help but notice how thick the fog was that made a quilt-like blanket over the entire community. Not only was the village in mourning, so was the land.

Alexelrod was the realtor to many spiritualist communities and traveled all over. He was liked by so many people.

If he had been murdered, as Gandolf believed, it could take months to visit all of those communities and interview potential suspects or witnesses. Unfortunately, murder wasn't good for a business community. Who would want to come to shop where there might be a murderer on the loose?

Though Gandolf was in charge, I still felt it was my duty to do a little investigating myself, only to see what I came up with.

There was a lot that I needed to do today, which was great because it would make my day go faster, and I was really looking forward to my Chinese takeout date with Oscar tonight.

I made a quick to-do list, but it became a to-see list before I headed off to work. Murderer or not, the village shops still had to open for business.

I glanced at my list one more time before I put it in my purse. Gerald and Raven were at the top. Each of them had seen something and neither wanted to tell.

I flung my bag over my shoulder and headed down the hill. Mr. Prince Charming darted in and out of the fog like he was chasing a string. The fog parted as he ran, leaving me a good path to see my way.

"Good fairy god-cat!" I yelled after him.

The fog might detour some of the tourists from coming into town, which would be fine with me since I had to get through my to-see list. I also wanted to keep working on a cure for Oscar. Plus I still had the "Mysteries and Magical Spells" book I had found outside of Ever After Books to thumb through before I gave it back to Ophelia.

Just as I was about to unlock the gate of A Charming Cure, I heard a little scuffle on the other side of the street, but couldn't see through the fog.

"June." Someone called out.

Instantly, a small circle of fog lifted and Ophelia was standing in the center.

"Hurry." Her eyes glowed red in a worrisome sort of way. She waved faster. "Now."

There was a purple orb floating to the right side of the gate in front of Ever After. The fog lifted with each step she took until she leapt into the orb, sending a swirl of gold like one of those childhood kaleidoscopes.

"Come on June." Ophelia's voice echoed into the air.

Without giving it much thought, I jumped through the small purple opening when the gold stopped spinning, landing right smack dab into what looked to be a bookstore. I quickly ducked when a book with wings flew right over my head.

"Oh my…" My mouth dropped when the book soared through the air and landed on a bookshelf right before another one took off, and then another, and another. It was like I was in the movie *Birds*, but it should be titled *Books*.

"As you can see," Ophelia's high-pitched voice was even higher. She lifted her hands in the air. "We have had a disturbance today and we don't do well with that."

"What disturbance and what kind of shop is this?" I was beginning to wonder if Alexelrod was right. Ever After

Books didn't belong in Whispering Falls. Or if I would have listened to him, he might be alive today.

The books swirled, dipped, and dove throughout the colorful shop. The wings of the books resembled the petals on the daisies in the flowerbed outside of the shop. There was a lamppost at the beginning of each aisle, filled with books.

In each corner of the store were big comfy couches with large fluffy pillows and baskets of snuggly blankets in all sorts of bright colors.

"It's my bookshop." She tossed her curls behind her head and walked ahead of me. "It's full of magic when no one who isn't spiritual is here."

I followed her, making sure to keep an eye out for the flying books.

"And I'm afraid it isn't looking too good for me or Ever After with that dreadful man found dead on my steps." She stopped, turned, and drummed her fingers. Her eyes narrowed and her back became ramrod straight. "Am I right?"

"Is this what you wanted to see me about?" I ducked, barely missing having my head detached.

"It is." She gestured for me to follow her. Her long black nails scraped the air.

"Alexelrod was hardly dreadful." I wanted to make sure that I made that clear with her, even though I was sure his dying wish was to run Ever After Books out of Whispering Falls. "You didn't know him. He was kind, thoughtful and very helpful to our community. It is I who should be questioning the reasons he didn't want your bookstore to open."

We proceeded to the back of the shop and through a door that opened up into Ophelia's office space, which wasn't much different than the actual shop. There were floor-to-ceiling shelves filled with books and a long black desk in the middle of the room.

"I have no idea why he didn't like me." She stopped in front of one of the bookshelves. "He is the one who came to my spiritual village after I asked for a realtor and he showed me this place. Then I moved and he went all crazy. Then he was murdered."

"Really?" Something just wasn't adding up.

"Yes," she said in a high-pitch voice. Her curls swayed back and forth as she nodded. "There are records of the entire transaction. But one of my books is missing and that is a key piece of evidence to his murder."

"You have thousands of books here." I pointed in the direction of the shop floor. "How could you possibly know that you are missing a book?"

The sign on the desk read *The Witch Is In*.

"I'm going to go out on a limb and say you're a witch." I pointed to her sign. "So snap your fingers and find the book."

"Yes. You already know that I'm a witch from yesterday when I was in your shop." She referred to the little incident at the store. "And you know they are going to go on a witch hunt because that man was found dead on my steps with the help of one of my books."

"I don't think I'd say that. There is no proof you killed..." I slapped my hand over my mouth. "Did you kill Alexelrod?"

"What do you think?" She stood with her hands firmly planted on her hips.

I was just about to tell her what I thought right before the bookstore door was busted down. We rushed out of her office to see what had happened. Gandolf bolted in with his gun drawn and waving around a book no bigger than the palm of my hand.

"By the order of the spiritual police in Whispering Falls, Ophelia Biblio, you are charged with the murder of Alexelrod Primrose." Another younger police officer, who I had never seen before, was standing behind him. He was rolling his eyes as Gandolf's baritone voice boomed, causing the books to go haywire. Everyone but Ophelia took cover. Gandolf ran behind a bookshelf and I hid behind him. I squeezed my eyes hoping nothing was going to whack me in the head.

"Stop!" Ophelia lifted her hands in the air. The books fell to the ground.

Once the coast was clear, Gandolf stepped out into the aisle waving the book like it was a white flag.

I reached into my bag without anyone seeing me and pulled out Madame Torres. Her hands were placed over her ears like she was trying to drown the craziness out.

"Listen to me." I shook her.

"Stop," she whispered. She could tell the severity of the situation. "I get motion sickness. Remember?"

"Sorry. But I need you to focus." I hunkered down and held her close to my face, almost eye-to-eye. "You have to get in touch with Mac McGurtle. Tell him to come to Ever After Books immediately."

Mac lived next to me in Locust Grove. Little did I knew that he was there to keep a spiritual eye on me. The village council sent him there to protect me in case I turned out to be a spiritualist. When they figured out that I did inherit my father's spiritual gifts, they sent Mr. Prince Charming to protect me. Little did I know that they were Spiritualists. I thought Mac was just the nosy neighbor and Mr. Prince Charming was a stray cat, until I found out otherwise after I moved to Whispering Falls.

Since he no longer had to take care of me, he had started to practice spiritual law again and he was the one

who helped me out of many crazy situations. I had no idea
what the book was all about, but I did know that my
intuition told me Ophelia didn't have anything to do with
Alexelrod's murder. But who did?

"Is this your book?" Gandolf's voice was courteous
but patronizing. He held the book up over his head in a
dramatic way. "Answer me!"

"Yes." Ophelia pinched her lips shut.

"Did you sell the book to anyone?" He continued to
barrage her with questions as he opened the book. It was
some sort of book you'd see, like a bracelet making book
where all the materials were attached to make a bracelet,
only this was about darts and it looked like the two darts
were missing from their place.

"Don't you dare answer his questions." Mac McGurtle
came through the door swiping the yellow crime scene tape
out of his way. "And it is not appropriate nor acceptable for
my client's store to remain closed."

"Who called you?" Gandolf pointed toward Mac, but
didn't wait for Mac's answer. He gestured for the new cop.
"Go on. Read her her rights."

"Ophelia Biblio…" the young officer's voice cracked
as he fiddled with the piece of paper as he started to read it.
"You have the right…"

"To open your shop!" Mac pushed his large black-
rimmed glasses up on his nose with his thick fingers. His
blue eyes zeroed in on the young officer like a vulture.
"That is what you have the right to do until you hear from
me. As for you, gentlemen," Mac put one arm around
Gandolf and another arm around the other officer and
started to walk them out of the shop. "Don't you have some
suspects to track down?"

"No more magic until you are cleared!" Gandolf
shouted, his face reddened and he jerked away from Mac.

"Rule Number Five in the bylaws state that you cannot leave the community until further notice."

"She won't." Mac assured them and then ripped the crime scene tape off the front door.

Ophelia's eyes turned black with a little gold ring around the rim. She didn't take her eyes off of Gandolf.

Suddenly Gandolf's belt completely unbuckled, giving way to his pants, exposing his tightie-whities. A sight that should never be seen by anyone's eyes.

He scrambled to pull them up.

"No magic!" He yelled galloping through the door and out of the shop.

The young officer's laughter had a sharp edge.

"Shut up!" Gandolf wasn't happy with his little minion's reaction.

"You bad witch." I couldn't help but love her wicked humor. "Did you make his pants fall down?"

Why did everyone have better powers than me? I was green with envy.

A faint smile crept up into her face, as her eyes relaxed into a sea-blue color. "I told you they are on a witch hunt."

Chapter Thirteen

I didn't know anything about a witch hunt, but I did know one thing, Ophelia did threaten Alexelrod earlier in the day. The early morning air was heavy with death as I left Mac and Ophelia alone to discuss the particulars of her case. Now I had to put Ophelia on my list of to-sees. That was going to have to wait until she was alone. She had something to tell me before Gandolf stormed in and I was going to find out what it was.

I felt my wrist for my charm bracelet. I had forgotten that Bella still had it since Mr. Prince Charming had gotten me a new wing charm. Visiting Bella to get my bracelet was now on the list of to-sees. And the day wasn't getting any longer.

Glorybee was lit up when I walked by. A nagging curiosity had me wondering about the change of heart Petunia had for Patience. I looked in the window.

Petunia stood in the back of the shop near the tall live tree where most of her animals took refuge when customers came in. The big Macaw was perched on her shoulder and she was hand feeding him. A couple of squirrels and chipmunks reared up on their legs to get a piece of whatever it was she had.

I knocked on the window to get her attention. When she saw me, she waved me in and I met her at the door.

"Get in here." She smiled, holding the door wide open. "You are out early this morning."

Get in here, get in here, squawk! The bird repeated. Repeating was something he was good at and thank goodness, he was. We had a little history together.

"I was on my way to get a jump on some extra work and saw your light was on. I had a few minutes to kill so I thought I'd say hi." I lied.

Hello! Hello! Squawk!

"Go on Clyde." Petunia shook her shoulder up and down. Clyde flew off to the highest branch in the tree.

"Clyde?" I questioned.

"I think his name is Clyde. At least he continues to say 'Clyde is a good boy.'" She straightened a few items on the shelves as we made our way back to the tree. "It's cleaning time."

She handed me a bucket with some brushes in it. I wasn't new to the routine. I had come over several times and helped her brush all the animals before leaving, because Mr. Prince Charming wouldn't leave the pet shop until he got his brushing.

We took a seat on the grass under the tree. One-by-one the animals made a single-file line, waiting patiently for their turn.

"I swear, this is the craziest thing I have ever seen." I couldn't help but smile as I brushed the stray cat that didn't budge when the squirrel ran by. "So tell me, what was with the change of heart at the meeting toward Petunia? I thought you wanted to sock it to her."

Petunia sat the brush down and pinned a falling piece of hair back up on top of her head. "Right before the meeting she told me that she thought the ostrich was a distant relative of hers and she was trying to figure out who it was."

"I thought you said these animals didn't have spiritual souls." I specifically remember when they showed up and she made the comment that they wouldn't communicate with her.

"I didn't think so." She shrugged and picked the brush back up. The hedgehog rolled over on his back with his legs up in the air. Petunia brushed his soft belly and quills just like she would brush a dog's fur. There was no difference between her animals. "What she said makes a lot of sense."

"What?" I had to know.

"The ostrich did love it down there and I caught him trying to go back several times after you found him there." The hedgehog ran off and the mallard duck made his way over with his life partner, the beaver. Petunia used a small brush to brush the beaver's teeth. "She said that his eyes possessed a particular look that was scared. He also was gentle with her and didn't peck her. The more I try to communicate with them, the closer to me they come."

I watched as she got up and started to smash her foot on the floor. I didn't know whether to take cover or laugh when Petunia threw her head back and starting making some really crazy noises.

Buzzecaw, buzzecaw, taw,taw,taw. Petunia continued to make strange noises as the animals rushed around her, landing at her feet, on her head, shoulders or any other part of her body that was flat enough to land on.

"See, I called for all the animals to come in animal language, not spiritual language." She nodded to the back of the room where the stray animals stood as if they didn't understand animal language.

Petunia lifted her hands and the animals scurried to where they had come from. After they were all situated, Petunia lifted her arms, closed her eyes, and chanted.

Guardians of the Dreamtime, Shapes and Forms.
Roots of the Mountain, Silent and Deep. Let it be known if
your soul is one to seek.

But the animals didn't budge.

"See!" She threw her hand back up in the air. "They don't respond to anything. I just don't get it. They have me baffled. And if Patience can get one of them to crack, it'll be worth it."

"Can't animals just be animals?" The only other animal I knew was Mr. Prince Charming and he definitely wasn't just an animal.

"No." She shook her head. "They are all different like you and me."

"Either way they should be responding to you, right?" I asked. I didn't really understand what she was saying.

"Haven't you listened to a word I have said?" Petunia fiddled with the string of hair that fell down the side of her face again. "Yes. Animals should respond, not just sit there."

I glanced back over at the animals. Each one of their beady little eyes stared at me. It would be fun to see what I could do to get them to talk. Any thinking of potions reminded me of Oscar which reminded me that A Charming Cure wasn't going to open itself and Oscar wasn't going to regain his memory with me hanging out with the animals.

The thought of sharing chopsticks with Oscar later made the butterflies in Glorybee float around me.

"Oscar?" Petunia asked.

"We are having dinner tonight." Excitement was written all over me. I waved my way out of the pet shop. The butterflies followed me up the street to A Charming Cure before they flew back to Glorybee.

Chapter Fourteen

"Hear ye, hear ye," Faith Mortimer's voice rang throughout Whispering Falls. I grabbed my Magical Cures Book from behind the counter, putting it down next to the cauldron. I wanted to hear if Faith had found out any more out about the murder. "If you have any information on the deadly attack against Alexelrod Primrose, please see Officer Gandolf at the police station. This headline was brought to you by The Gathering Grove Tea Shoppe. If you need an afternoon pick-me-up, come check out the new selection of chai teas and be sure to tell Gerald Reguila that you heard it in the Gazette."

Gerald, I tapped my list that was sitting on the counter. Mr. Prince Charming lifted his head off the stool where he had planted himself as soon as we opened the shop.

Mewl, mewl. His little white head bobbed up and down as if he knew exactly what I was thinking.

"Good idea." Madame Torres was deep in my bag that was hanging on the back of the stool.

I swiped my hand down Mr. Prince Charming's body before putting my hand in the bag to retrieve my snarky crystal ball.

"Good morning." I smiled at her. By the blue color of her face, I could see that she wasn't happy. "What?"

"You couldn't have said 'good morning Madame Torres' earlier when you summoned me to find Mac McGurtle? I would have appreciated it." Her eyes and lips were the same blue. There were red puffs of air emitted with every word spoken.

"Are you telling me that you are mad because I asked you to do your job?" Why did I get the crystal ball with the smart aleck button? I put her next to the cauldron. "Need I remind you that I could drop your fancy little glass ball off at a flea market at any time and you would never be able to speak again?"

Madame Torres face disappeared. The inside swirled black and grey with flecks of red sparking out right before the ball went black. I knew I would make her mad with my comment, but she knew the rules. Crystal balls did pick their owner. In the entire Universe, there was only one owner per crystal ball unless they were in the owner's will and she knew it. Therefore, it was "do what I say," or risk my getting rid of her.

"Besides, I'm still mad that you felt the need to put me on Make-Me-A-Match." I had to get the last word in.

Of course I would never get rid of her, but threatening her, to put her in her place, did make me happy.

The clock chimed nine am, letting me know it was time to unlock the front door and seeing Gerald for an afternoon tea break was exactly what I needed.

Letting out a heavy sigh, I realized that I got nothing accomplished on Oscar's potion. The line of customers at the door told me that it was going to be a long day.

Before walking over to the door, I grabbed one of the Mojo Bags that I didn't have time to give out at the council meeting. The shop hadn't been cleansed since Alexelrod's death and I wanted to make sure to keep any awful spirits out. Especially today. Nothing could go wrong. Nothing was going to keep me from my date with Oscar.

"Spirits and souls wherever you go, send up the light on A Charming Cure shop site." I waved the protection Mojo Bag in the air. I grabbed an apron from the hook, tied it around my waist on my way to unlock the front door and then proceeded down the steps to unlock the ornamental gate.

"Good morning!" I greeted the line of eager customers. I stepped aside to let them walk in. I smiled at each one as they walked by. "Welcome to A Charming Cure."

"Whoo hoo! June!" Bella waved my charm bracelet in the air. It swayed back and forth from her fingertips.

I waved. It was great seeing her, but the bracelet made me feel a lot better.

"I'm glad you are here. I had you on my to-see list." If only the others would come over, then my list would be complete. That was just too easy, though.

"I wanted to get this to you ASAP since the 'you-know-what.'" She tensed her jaws causing her lips to part and exposing the gap between her two front teeth.

"Alexelrod?" I ran my hands down my slick bob, noticing that it was getting a little too long and I probably should have made an appointment with Chandra over at A Cleansing Spirit Spa before my date tonight. But it was too late now.

"No." The crease between her brows deepened. "The curse of the first Village President's meeting."

"What curse?" Stunned, I stood there and let her clasp my bracelet around my wrist. I rubbed the new air element charm between my finger and thumb. Curse was never a good word to hear, especially in the spiritual world.

"When there is an interruption on the first meeting of the new Village President, it sets the precedent for a bad first year." Bella couldn't even look at me when she told me the awful news. News that would stick with me for the entire year.

"I wouldn't consider Alexelrod's death an interruption. I'd consider that a crisis." I half joked, but knew that I was in trouble. "What do I need to do to make sure this curse is broken?"

"Unfortunately, there isn't anything. Just make sure that no matter what comes your way, you go with the flow and handle it. And I mean *everything*."

"*Everything*?"

"Yes, everything. Including complaints about your love life."

Love life? My heart skipped a couple of beats. I grabbed the gate and leaned into it, hoping it would catch my fall.

Chapter Fifteen

"She does this all the time." A familiar voice echoed in my ear. Oscar's sweet voice was music to my ears. "June, wake up."

I needed to hear his voice a little longer so I kept my eyes closed.

"Here, use this," Raven Mortimer said.

"Is that a generic Ding Dong?" Oscar asked.

"Generic?" Raven was not pleased. "Let me tell you something, Oscar Park. Just because you lost..."

I jumped up, realizing I was on my couch in my cottage.

"What happened?" I pretended to act like I didn't remember the curse, and I had to stop Raven from telling Oscar about his memory loss. He would never accept the fact that I was a spiritualist. I glared at Raven. Her dark lashes cast shadows down her cheeks.

Never make a Dark-Sider mad had always been my motto. I grabbed the June's Gem from her hand and stuffed it in my mouth.

"Those must do the trick." Oscar smiled and rocked back and forth on his heels. He was dressed in civilian clothes. His dark hair had been freshly cut and shaved a little closer up the back. His beautiful eyes danced as he watched me scarf down the tasty treat.

"These are delicious." My words were muffled from the mouthful of goodness. "How did I get here?"

I sat down on the couch and laid my head on the pillow. There were small Chinese containers on the coffee table.

"What time is it?" Had I been blacked out for the whole day?

"I don't know." Oscar shrugged and pointed to Raven. "I just got here for our dinner and found her with you here. I didn't know that you were still blacking out. Is it the nightmares again?"

I shook my head. I used to have nightmares that predicted the future, but since moving to Whispering Falls, those had stopped.

"Bella said you passed out when she told you about the curse." Raven picked at her black fingernails and shifted to one side.

"Curse?" Oscar laughed.

"Oh that." I laughed and waved her off. "Bella said that there had never been a shop that was prosperous in A Charming Cure's location."

Raven's mouth flew open and quickly shut when I gave her the stink eye. She didn't really know what was going on with Oscar, and I wasn't about to tell either of them at that moment.

"Yeah, that's it." Sarcasm dripped from her mouth. "I'm out of here. Good seeing you again, Oscar. And June, don't forget to send Eloise a Thank You Gram for running your shop today."

"You too." He didn't pay her too much attention as she left the cottage. Mr. Prince Charming darted in before she shut the door and jumped on top of me, sniffing my nose. Oscar rubbed down his back and picked him off me, putting him on the floor.

Rowr! Hiss, hiss! Mr. Prince Charming gnashed his teeth and batted the air toward Oscar. They were never big fans of each other. Both were jealous of the other for two completely different reasons.

Mr. Prince Charming knew my innermost and deepest feelings for Oscar, and Oscar knew how much I wanted a cat when I was a little girl. When Mr. Prince Charming showed up when I was ten, I didn't go anywhere without him.

"He's so protective for a cat." Oscar grabbed the chopsticks and snapped them apart and rubbed them together before he picked up one container of food. "You ready to eat?"

"I'm starving." I glanced at the clock. I couldn't believe I had passed out and stayed out all day. The news of the curse still made my head hurt, not to mention my heart. I sat up and reached for a carton of Chinese food.

"What happened to make you pass out? Were you working?"

He was throwing a bunch of questions at me that I couldn't answer. All I gathered was that someone notified Eloise that I passed out and she came to keep the shop open, which was strange in itself. Eloise kept to herself in her treehouse deep in the woods and her morning cleansing of the community was enough involvement for her. But that could have been because of the past rules, which didn't let all spiritualists live in Whispering Falls, and that included Dark-Siders which was what Eloise was.

"I was talking to another shop owner and that's the last thing I remember."

"It was nice of them to run the shop so you didn't lose money." He stuffed his mouth with a crab Rangoon.

I smiled and reached for another container to take a bite out of it. That was our thing. Oscar and I would order loads of Chinese food and take bites out of each carton.

"I wanted to know if you want to come over for dinner at my place tomorrow night. I have something very important to tell you."

My insides tingled with excitement. My mind twirled with the idea of a romantic dinner for two. Candles, wine, champagne, and a little lip-locking included. The thought of being in his arms again sent sheer delight throughout my bones.

"Of course." I immediately knew I would change any plans that I had, but at the moment my brain was too mushy seeing hearts to even think about my schedule. *Go with the flow,* I recalled Bella saying about the curse, and the…love thing.

The night went by too fast. There was no touching or kissing, which would have been my choice of dessert, but it was too soon for that. I was going to have to establish a romantic relationship like I had done a year ago and gently tell him about the spiritualist thing.

"Don't forget tomorrow night." Oscar didn't need to remind me. That was the only thing on my mind. He opened the door. Like a spotlight, the moon beamed down on him giving him a mysterious glow, or maybe it was my imagination of his magical powers over me even though he possessed no magical powers.

"I'll be there." I leaned on the door, and reached out to touch his arm.

"Okay." His brows lifted in surprise at my gesture. He backed away with a confused look on his face. "I'll see you tomorrow night."

I shut the door behind him and pressed my back up against it.

"You don't know it now, but you are madly in love with me." I looked over at the glow coming from my bag that was hanging on one of the kitchen chairs. I was glad to see that Raven had brought it home from the shop.

Madame Torres must have had something to say. It better be an apology. I reached in and grabbed her.

"I'm assuming you are going to apologize." I held her up, but squinted to read the words that had replaced her face in the globe.

It was some sort of spreadsheet with names and numbers.

"Bill, 5553434, Joe, 5558903, Evan..." The list went on and on.

"These are your matches from Make-Me-A-Match." Madame Torres's voice could be heard, but she was not seen. "Who knew men were so desperate for a date?"

"You have got to be joking me?" My voice was harsh with frustration. Madame Torres knew how to turn a great evening into a terrible one. I threw her in my bag, knowing the mid-air flight would make her sick to her stomach. I took my bag and flung it over my shoulder.

"Let's go." I held the door open for Mr. Prince Charming and made sure to lock and close it after he darted out.

I stomped down the hill. I was sure there was steam coming out of my ears. Madame Torres needed to be put in her place, and I was too new to this spiritualist stuff to even know how to discipline her.

The fireflies darted in and out in front of me. They were the souls of teenagers, and like teenagers, they only came out at night and stayed up until the sun came up, sleeping all day.

"Go on." I shooed them away. Surely, they had better things to do than bother me. But they wanted to tease Mr. Prince Charming who batted at them before knocking a couple of them down. Luckily, he didn't hurt them, because Petunia would be all over me.

In a couple of minutes, I was in the gate and inside A Charming Cure. It looked like there were a lot of sales while I was gone by the empty tables and shelves, which meant I had a long night ahead of me.

Chapter Sixteen

"I wondered how long it would take you to get here."
A voice from the back scared me until the light flipped on.
Eloise was sitting on the stool that butted up to the counter,
drumming her fingers next to my cauldron.

"You scared me." I held my hand to my heart. "I can't
thank you enough for taking over today."

Mr. Prince Charming beat me to her. He was already in
her lap giving her all sorts of nose bumps. He loved her just
as much as I did. With Mr. Prince Charming between us, I
still hugged her.

"How is my nephew?" Her voice cracked when she
asked. Tears sat on the edge of her bottom eyelid. One big
crocodile tear rolled down her face when she blinked. The
hurt was so deep that I could feel her pain.

"He is good. In fact the same as before we knew we
were spiritualists and before we were an item." At least I
got to talk to Oscar, where as Eloise can't hug him or even
tell him that she's his aunt when he'd love to have family.
Plus, Rule Number Six in the Whispering Falls Rule Book
said that you can't tell a non-spiritualist that you are a
spiritualist.

"But…" She drew her brows up to the sky, and then
glanced at the cauldron.

"So I miss him too and I'm going to find a way to
bring Sorcerer Oscar back." Now I felt like I was going to
cry. "I can't live with myself knowing that he was truly
meant to be someone else. Someone other than Oscar Park,
Locust Grove police officer."

A few minutes went by without either of us saying a
word and I took the moment to gather my emotions and fill
the tables back up with new inventory.

"It was busy today." Eloise helped bring some boxes up front and restock some of the bath products. "Many of your customers asked for you."

"That's good." It was always good to know there were repeat customers. "I can't believe that I was passed out for so long."

I straightened some of the diet supplements. I was a stickler about the front of the bottle always facing the front. It was a ghost from the past really. Darla was so messy and I was the complete opposite.

"It's times like this that I miss your mom." Eloise stopped and stared out the window. The full moon acted as a flashlight over top of Whispering Falls. It was beautiful the way the ornamental gates in front of the shops glistened in a magical way.

"Me too." I smiled. Darla would have loved the fact that I came back to Whispering Falls and embraced my gift.

"Let's stop by Ever After Books tomorrow and see about that book club I wanted to start." Eloise grabbed the little feather duster I kept behind the counter and started to dust all the shelves and bottles. It was the last thing I had to do before I got cracking on the potion.

"Sounds great." If I couldn't have Darla, Eloise was the next best thing. I flipped the switch on the cauldron and then turned to my intuition as I went down the line of ingredients, tapping each one.

Crimson Nimroot was good for damaged health and it couldn't hurt to add a pinch. The Nightshade and Skeeter Tail made my intuition radar go off, so I grabbed those.

The way I figured, I had nothing to lose. The more ingredients the better. And if anyone snitched on me for making the potion and I got banned, oh well, I could be happy living with Oscar for the rest of my life.

"It's all clean." Eloise turned a blind eye to what I was doing. "Come over and get some fresh ingredients from the garden. I have a new batch popping up."

"I will!" I hollered out from behind the petition. I wasn't going to waste any more time. I wanted the potion ready for tomorrow night. I knew I could slip some in the champagne I was dreaming about.

Chapter Seventeen

The cauldron was bubbling full force and I was just
about to put in the Charred Skeever Hide that I knew was
going to bring Oscar back his memory when someone
knocked on the door.

Mewl. Mr. Prince Charming's head turned and he
jumped up and dashed to the door.

Tap, tap, tap. The knock was followed by a flashlight
beam dancing around the window of the shop. Mr. Prince
Charming darted around and pawed at the light as if it were
a cicada.

"Who is it?" I rubbed my hands on my apron and
looked up at the clock. It was well past ten pm.

"It's Sheriff Lance," the unfamiliar voice called out
into the night. "Are you okay in there?"

I unlocked the door and pulled it open. The young
officer that was with Gandalf earlier at Ever After Books
stood on the other side.

"I'm fine, Sheriff." I ran my hands through my bob.
After fooling around with potions and bending over the
cauldron, I was sure I was a mess. I noticed the light was
still on at The Gathering Grove Tea Shoppe. Since Gerald
was on my list of to-sees, I suddenly had a hankering for
some sleepy time tea. All I had to do was get rid of Sheriff
Lance. "Is something wrong?"

"Colton Lance." Colton took his hat off, revealing a
nice messy head of blond hair. He stuck his hand out. "I'm
the Sheriff in training. We weren't introduced properly in
the bookstore."

"You are the new sheriff in training?" There was
something off about this whole situation. Who hired him?
Oscar was going to come right back and claim his post as
soon as I gave him the potion. "I'm June Heal, the Village

President. Don't you think I should know something about this officer in training thing?" I ran my pointer finger up and down.

"I guess you are going to have to ask Officer Gandolf about that." He shrugged. His eyes glanced over my shoulder. "I'm patrolling at night to make sure that nothing funny is going on with the murder and all."

I looked behind me to see exactly what had him mesmerized. There was smoke billowing out from behind the partition.

"Damn!" I dashed back to the cauldron. The potion had bubbled over, leaving the cauldron with very little potion left. I flipped off the cauldron switch and grabbed a roll of paper towels.

"Are you sure everything is okay?" Colton had stepped just inside the shop with his hand on his holster as though he was going to be involved in a showdown.

"Yes!" I yelled from behind the counter. "I was making new inventory when you knocked and didn't turn down the temperature."

I lied. There was no new inventory or temperature controls on a cauldron. The ingredients and intention of the cure were all the cauldron needed to know to magically make the potion. Besides, he probably didn't understand cauldrons or wouldn't even know what I was talking about.

"Come on in. I'm sorry, I've lost my manners." I blew my bangs out of my eyes and threw a fistful of paper towels in the trash.

Colton came on in like he had nothing else going on. His six-foot-three or so frame looked like it was in good shape, and his big brown eyes turned down just a tad at the corner, giving him that sweet puppy dog look. Much different from Oscar. In fact, he was much bigger in size – not in height, but more muscular than Oscar.

"Are you a Homeopathic Spiritualist?" He asked. The bottle he picked up was for menstrual cramps. I smiled.

"I am." I walked over and tapped the bottle in his hand. "Unless you are a woman, I don't think that is going to work for you."

His laugh was deep, warm, and rich. I brought my hand up to stifle my giggle, but it was too late, literally. I couldn't stop laughing because he was laughing.

Mr. Prince Charming danced around Colton's feet doing his signature figure-eight move. Colton bent down and picked him up.

My jaw dropped. Mr. Prince Charming didn't like any guy around me.

"Hey, buddy." Colton bent down and found Mr. Prince Charming's sweet spot right behind his ears, giving him a good scratch.

Purr, purr. I swear Mr. Prince Charming grinned. I gave him the stink eye.

"What a great cat." He gave him a few more ear rubs before Mr. Prince Charming was ready to get down.

"He is." Sarcasm dripped from my lips. There was something strange going on here. I knew Mr. Prince Charming was up to something. "He's a nosy old thing."

"Aw," Colton blew me off. "All cats are curious. I have one myself. So you are a . . ."

"Homeopathic shop." I smiled taking in the atmosphere I had created. I was very proud of A Charming Cure and how well it had blossomed over the past year.

"My mom is going to love coming here." He walked around picking up a few bottles here and there. "She's an Intuitist and Curist?"

"Me too!" There was excitement bubbling inside. I had never met anyone else like me. "I hope she comes to visit."

"As a matter of fact," he pulled up the cuff of his uniform sleeve and glanced at his watch, "she will be here in about nine hours."

"Very cool. Where are you from?" I followed him around as he browsed the shop. There were so many things that I didn't understand about my gift and I'd love to pick his mother's brain.

"We are transferring from the village out West." He nodded like I knew where he was talking about, but I didn't. "This job came available and I came out here to interview and put Officer Gandolf in place as an interim."

That made a lot of sense. All of the swapping out of Oscar to Gandolf was around the time I was appointed Village President and Izzy Solstice was still in charge. She would be able to give me all the details of when Gandolf was leaving and Colton would be taking over.

"I hope you like it here." I ran my hand along a couple of tables as we passed. Eloise must've missed a little lint when she was dusting.

"I'm sure I will. It was great until the big murder."

"What is the latest on that?" That wasn't prying. I was the president and needed to know.

"Since you are authorized in the investigation," he lowered his voice, "there was a trace of poison found on the ends of the darts. And the book that the poison instructions came from was from Ever After Books, which puts Ophelia Biblio as our number one suspect."

"Oh." Suddenly I was regretting getting Mac involved in the case. I walked up to the counter and shuffled a few things around. The cauldron was a mess and I wasn't looking forward to cleaning it. On second thought, it hadn't been working all that great since Ophelia put it back together and a new one would be nice. It would go on my list of things to get when I made it over to Wands, Potions, and Beyond.

"We checked out the records of all the books sold and no one bought that book." He leaned up against the counter. Our eyes met. He smiled. I looked away.

Meow, meow. Mr. Prince Charming pranced around the shop with his tail waving in the air. I almost wanted to strangle him.

"There was one thing that didn't add up." He shuffled his feet.

"And what was that?" My intuition told me that he was holding something back.

"I shouldn't say anything because I didn't even mention it to Gandolf yet." He bit the corner of his lip.

"I'm not going to say anything. We have to work together." I encouraged him to tell me, not because I had to know, but because I was curious.

"Gandolf is old school Crystallamancy." He referred to Gandolf's spiritual ability to read crystal balls, which would tie the link between Izzy and Gandolf. I bet they were old friends from crystal ball school and she was in a pinch to have a new sheriff so she probably called on her old friend. "He sees things black and white."

I nodded.

"He thinks Ophelia had to have killed Mr. Primrose because the book was from her shop, the darts were found in front of her shop, where she and Mr. Primrose just so happened to have had a big public fight." His voice dropped. His eyes dipped down with concern. "See, that is where he isn't seeing the broader picture."

"You have to admit his logic is good." When Colton presented the facts, they did point right at Ophelia.

"Now you aren't looking at the broader picture." He tapped his finger on the counter. "Ophelia is not a Dark-

Sider. She's a Good-Sider witch. She has no use for the darts."

"And she wouldn't have been able to get her hands on some poison." My eyes flew up and out the window as I thought about all the impossibilities of Ophelia killing Alexelrod. "She couldn't have just turned him into a frog."

Frog? Animals? Did Colton hit on something? I bit my lip trying to concentrate on him but my head played pictures of the stray animals. Ophelia and the strays were the only two new things in Whispering Falls and they showed up about the same time. And I couldn't help but feel that there was some sort of connection to the two, but what?

"Right, but..." he shook his head, "there is more. There is a dart missing from the book and I'm afraid the killer is going to strike again."

"Missing? You said that the book had two darts and that was exactly what was found at the scene." I recalled seeing the book high above Gandolf's head when he had confronted Ophelia and seeing the two darts were missing, but not a third.

"Right. Two darts. One of the darts didn't fit in the space the book provided. We only found one of the darts to have a poison tip and it wasn't the dart that came from the book, which means that someone had different darts with a more powerful punch to do the job and frame Ophelia. Someone who knew exactly what they were doing."

"You are telling me that someone is framing Ophelia Biblio, and they are still out there?" I tried to keep control as the fear of a killer on the loose knotted in my stomach.

Slowly he nodded his head up and down. The words eerily dripped from his lips, "That is exactly what I'm telling you."

"Did you question Faith Mortimer?" That was a valid question. Not that I was accusing her, but it did seem fair to ask in case she saw someone running from the scene of the crime. "I'm no detective or anything, but did she see anyone other than Alexelrod?"

"Gandolf is in charge of the investigation since I'm in training, but he said that he questioned everyone at the scene and everyone came up clean."

What Colton was telling me didn't send my gut into radar, but what Colton didn't tell me did give me some questions. My intuition told me that something about the whole investigation was missing. But what?

Did they ask Faith the right questions? It wouldn't hurt to pay her a visit and get her to do a cover story on Ever After Books. That way, I'd be able to ask her some things without her being suspicious.

The cure I had started for Oscar would be fine in the cauldron over night. The concoction was just a simple power booster for an existing spiritualist. I had yet to add the memory portion of the cure. It was getting late, and I didn't want Gerald to leave the shop before I spoke to him.

Chapter Eighteen

After countless times of telling Colton I was fine and that I would be fine going home alone even this late at night, he finally left reluctantly. If it had been Oscar not wanting to leave me, then it would have been a different story, and I might have played the defenseless shop owner with the big bad killer on the loose. There was nothing telling me that someone was out to get me.

I was going to make sure that Gerald answered my tea-reading questions.

I gathered all my stuff, including a light sweater because the air had a chill to it along with Madame Torres. With A Charming Cure locked up tight and Mr. Prince Charming at my side, we headed down Main Street to The Gathering Grove.

Rowl! Mr. Prince Charming reared up on his hind-legs and batted into the air before he darted off in the opposite direction of the teashop.

"Chicken," I murmured. There was nothing there to make him run off, or so I thought. "Some fairy god-cat you are!" I hollered after him.

A cloud drifted in front of the moon, leaving Whispering Falls in complete darkness, except for the small light at The Gathering Grove.

"Keep your eye on the light," I whispered, fending off any fear creeping up in my soul, and threw my sweater around my shoulders to warm the chill bumps, pinching the collar up around my neck. I had a sneaky suspicion that I was not alone. It wasn't my intuition that gave me the hint, but the twigs cracking under some heavy footsteps.

My legs worked overtime without me even telling them to do so as I rushed down the sidewalk, but they

turned to jell-o when a flashlight made a spotlight on my
face and a hand reached out squeezing my shoulder.
    I froze.
    "What are you doing out here?" Officer Gandolf's
voice boomed out into the night.
    "Thank goodness." I put my hand to my heart to steady
the beating and slow my breathing. "You scared me to
pieces."
    "You should be at home where it's safe." He didn't
leave any room to argue. He took his hand off my shoulder.
    "I was cleaning up my shop and thought I'd grab a cup
of sleepy time tea from Gerald before heading home." I
was a bit relieved that Gandolf and Colton were taking this
murder seriously.
    "Hurry up. We don't need another member of the
community dead." He didn't need to remind me.
    "But..." I wanted to ask him a few questions about
Faith, but my gut told me to go and not do it tonight. I also
wanted to know why they were looking for a killer if he
was so sure Ophelia Biblio had done it.
    "But what?" His voice was strong, steady, and loud.
    "Nothing. I'm going now." I pointed toward the
teashop and practically ran to The Gathering Grove.
    I found the door locked when I turned the handle.
Apparently, Gerald was just as freaked out as I was about
the strange happenings in Whispering Falls, because we
never locked our doors if we were in our stores. I jiggled
the handle to try again with no luck.
    Knock, knock, knock. Gerald emerged from the storage
room in the back of the shop with a handful of to-go coffee
mugs piled up in his arms. He nodded when he saw me and
came over after he placed the cups behind the counter.
    "It's late." He opened the door. "What are you doing
here?"

He didn't step aside or even try to hold the door open for me to come in.

"Can I come in?"

"I'm a little busy." He looked behind him as though he was expecting someone to walk out of the storage closest any minute. "Can it wait until tomorrow?"

I looked up and down Main Street before I pulled my sweater back up around my ears to block out the chill. I made sure I didn't see Gandolf. "Actually I really wanted to talk to you about the tea leaf reading. I think something was in it and you didn't want to tell me."

"You might as well come on in." There was resignation in his voice. He stepped aside. When I walked in, he popped his head outside and looked both ways before he quickly shut and locked the door behind me. "There were some things that I didn't want to say in front of Faith or Alexelrod. It had to do with the leaves lying past the handle."

Gerald went behind the counter and pulled out the cup that Alexelrod had drank from. The leaves were still plastered all over the inside.

"I don't see anything in that mess." I shrugged when he tilted the cup toward me. Faith Mortimer made me jump when she walked out from the storage area since I didn't know anyone else was there.

At first, I thought maybe Gerald was cheating on Petunia with Faith, but Faith quickly cleared that up.

"June!" There were tears dripping down her face. "Are you here to help?"

"Help?" I was more confused than ever.

"I haven't told her anything yet. We were trying to get it cleared up without involving you since you are the Village President," Gerald said. He set the cup on the counter and pulled up two chairs, one for me and one for Faith. "Have a seat."

While we sat down, Gerald went back over to the storefront windows, pulled down the blinds and closed them.

"What is going on?" There was a sick feeling twirling around my stomach. Either they were going to tell me something bad, or they were going to tell me something and as the president, I would have to turn that information over to Gandolf.

"The cup says that I'm involved with Alexelrod's murder." There was a worried look in Faith's deep-set blue eyes. She ran her fingers through her long blond hair. "I swear I didn't do anything. I stood on the outskirts of the meeting waiting for Alexelrod to show up. I needed to get a good scoop for fear of..." Her voice drifted off before she started to sob uncontrollably.

Gerald wrapped his arms around her like a loving father, stroking her hair, telling her it was going to be okay.

My mind tried to stay focused on my gut feelings and less on the facts Faith was telling me. Nothing was coming to me.

"Did Gandolf ask you about it?" I asked. If I recalled correctly, Colton had said that she was cleared from questioning.

"He asked me a few things."

"Did he arrest you?" That was the most important question.

"No." She shook her head.

"Then why are you worried?" Not that blowing off the tealeaves was a good idea, but sometimes spiritualists get things wrong. Sometimes the recipient could change the outcome of their lives by doing something different from what they had originally planned.

"The leaves say I am involved in the murder." She pointed to the cup and pulled away like it was a snake about to bite her.

There was no calming her down.

"Gerald?" I needed to hear it straight from the expert.

He paced back and forth with his hands clasped behind his back. *Ahem,* he cleared his throat. "The leaves I used were carefully chosen to figure out Alexelrod's state of mind." I continued to watch Gerald as he seemed to go to a faraway place. He almost made me dizzy watching him walk the same pattern back and forth. With his head held high, he never once blinked or looked at us. He just stared straight ahead with each foot stepping directly in front of the other. "He was of sound mind when he was protesting. The protest had nothing to do with Ophelia Biblio. The protest had everything to do with a book that was there. The leaves said the book in question was no longer at Ever After Books. Though it did not tell of Alexelrod's death, it did tell of Faith Mortimer being involved in the scene."

He continued to ramble on, ignoring what was going on around us. Faith was sobbing, I wanted to ask some questions, but he wasn't mentally present. He was doing a reading, which brought most spiritualists outside of the physical world. I knew nothing about it, but have witnessed it by watching the various spiritualists in Whispering Falls. It was like they were in a trance of some sort. Again...I only *wished* I had those kinds of gifts.

"See?" Faith blew her nose in a Gathering Grove napkin.

"It doesn't prove anything unless you are guilty."

Faith's head shot up. "You think I killed him don't you!"

"What would be your reason for killing him?"

"To get more ratings for the paper. People do many things when they are desperate." Gerald snapped out of his trace.

"What did you say?" There was a sudden urge for me to hear exactly what he had said.

"I'm not desperate!" Faith jumped up from the chair she was sitting in.

"What are you talking about?" Gerald reached out for the counter and held on. He was a little wobbly on his feet, so I offered him the chair Faith had been sitting in. The last thing I needed to have to do was take care of Faith and Gerald.

"You insinuated that she might have killed Alexelrod because she was desperate to get some subscribers to boost sales due to the downturn in the economy." The words did make a lot of sense.

It was a lot to think about. If Faith's job were in jeopardy because of budget cuts, following a murder investigation would get a lot more subscribers, which would turn the cuts away from the paper. As it stood now, the paper was the first thing to go.

"I did?" Gerald drew back. "I had no idea what all I said. It takes everything out of me nowadays to do a leaf-reading. I read what the spirit tells me."

His vacant eyes glanced over at Faith. That was all she needed to hear before she bolted out of the door.

"It looks like this investigation has only begun." Gerald twirled the edges of his mustache. "The reading also showed a new officer is in town."

"Colton?"

"You know him?" Gerald questioned me.

"Not really." *Only that he was muscular, hot, and hunky* I thought. But I wasn't looking. "He stopped by the shop tonight to see if I was okay."

"What do we really know about him? Did you hire him? Did Gandolf?" Gerald threw a lot of questions at me that I couldn't answer. I had only assumed Izzy had taken part in the hiring since she was part of Oscar being fired.

I wasn't about to tell Gerald that Colton was doing his own investigating. Nor did I say anything about the darts.

"About the reading." I wanted to get back to more of the concrete stuff that we knew about. "The book you referred to, was it the one with the darts?"

"Oddly enough, no. The dart book wasn't even in his tea-reading." He tapped the back of his neck, right under the ear lobe, about where the dart hit Alexelrod. "There was a skull and crossbones over top of Faith's name, which doesn't fare well for her."

My throat tightened. Even though Faith wasn't named a suspect, the odds weren't looking good. She had motive with the looming cuts to the paper and she was clearly upset, which could mean that she knew they were close to figuring out she did do it.

"I'm afraid the leaves say we have a murderer on the loose." Gerald had that same faraway look in his eye as he had earlier. "And it will shake our village."

"How?" I asked.

"I'm not sure." His eyes glazed over yet again. His next words shook me to my core. "The animals in town are up to no good. I tried to tell my sweet Petunia, but she doesn't want to believe it."

"Do the animals have something to do with the killer?" My conversation with Colton about Ophelia being a good witch rushed into my thoughts like a raging hurricane. If Gerald said that the killer and the animals are tied, I was going to have to go to Gandolf with the information that Colton was hiding.

"I don't know," Gandolf whispered. He shook his head. His expression turned to stone.

After I had made it home safely, I checked and re-checked the locks on my cottage door. For the first time, I could honestly say that I was scared. A dart could come flying out from anywhere at any time and we'd never know who'd sent it flying.

I tried to keep calm and think about other things like Oscar, but Gerald's last words spooked me to my core.

Chapter Nineteen

I barely slept at all and woke up early. There was no sense in delaying the day and putting off talking to Gandolf any longer. There were questions I had and had a right to know.

The sun peeked through the cracks of the window blinds, which meant that I could walk down the hill in daylight, which was much different than walking in the dark with a killer on the loose. Without further delay, I pulled my scared self out from underneath the blankets and sat on the edge of the bed.

"This dart thing didn't bother you," I said to Mr. Prince Charming who was curled at the end of the bed. "And don't think I didn't know what you were up to last night either with Officer Colton."

"It looks like I don't have to renew your profile on Make-Me-A-Match." Madame Torres appeared in the crystal ball. She wore an emerald green turban with a yellow stone in the middle, and eye shadow to match.

"What does that mean?" I asked firmly. I knew what it meant, but I wasn't going to give her the pleasure of admitting to knowing. When I went into the bathroom to get ready, I could hear her rattling off Colton's stats like we were at a baseball game.

"Colton Lance, tall, blonde, handsome, muscular, from a spiritualist family. He loves family and hanging out. Colton has had one serious girlfriend who cheated on him two years ago. Since then, he has thrown himself into his job." She barely took a breath. "Did I mention how hunky he is? And single?"

"You did." I swabbed some lip-gloss on my lips and put the tube in my jeans pocket. "Did I mention that I'm having dinner with Oscar tonight?"

"Did you notice that Oscar doesn't even know the real you?"

"Oscar knows perfectly well who I am." Deep down I knew she was right, but that was all about to change. "With my new ideas for a cure, we will be back to normal in no time."

"Have you ever thought that you aren't supposed to make a cure for him?"

"Why would you say that?"

"Because you have not had this much trouble with a potion since you burned down your shed in your previous life." Madame Torres reminded me of my last mortal days in Locust Grove.

"I'm not having problems with a cure." Admitting to being stuck was not something I was willing to do. That seemed along the lines of failure and I wasn't about to give up on Oscar. "I've got one part down, now I'm going to do the next one."

There were two things that were going to help me. One was Aunt Helena and the other had to be written in the book I smuggled out of the bushes of Ever After Books.

I went to the kitchen to get the book out of my bag and realized I had put it behind the counter at A Charming Cure.

Just then, there was a knock at the door. I rushed over to see who it was.

"June, the inevitable has happened." Faith was bent over, panting, out of breath. Her pale skin was almost haunting. "They might as well put me in jail. I have nothing to live for anymore."

"What's wrong?"

"Gandolf told me that more than likely, this week was going to be my last week for the Gazette."

"What?" How did Gandolf know anything about the budget cuts? He was the interim sheriff, not the president. It was definitely time to get some answers around here.

"He told me they were going to have to bring in more officers to aid in the investigation and to be prepared to stop production of the paper." She didn't seem as upset as she was the night before.

"You know what." I bit the corner of my lip. I was about to say something that I might regret, but I needed the time to go see some of the people on my to-see list and this was the only way I saw my list getting completed. "Don't you worry about the Gazette. I haven't heard anything about it. Can you work in the shop for me today? I have a ton of things to get done."

I knew it wasn't a fabulous job to help her "gift" but it was a paying job. Besides, A Charming Cure was doing so much business, it was about time to hire someone.

"June!" Faith squealed. "I'd love to! Thank you, thank you, thank you!" She threw her arms around my neck so tight that my head nearly popped right off my shoulders.

"No problem. I was just about to go down for the day." I pried her off me and went back to get my bag. "You can follow me and I can show you the ropes."

In a few minutes, we were at the shop. There wasn't much to teach her. She had already run Wicked Good's cash register, which was about the same. Plus, the bottles had prices on them. The only thing different was the extra-added ingredients, and those could be classified as special orders. Faith had a good enough intuition with her gift of Clairaudience that she would know when a client needed a true personal cure.

"Did you see a book about spells around here?" I was bent behind the counter looking for the "Mysteries and

Magical Spells" book that I had found under the bushes in front of Ever After Books.

"No." Faith was going around all the tables straightening the tablecloths and making sure the bottles were facing out. Even though I had done that last night, it was still good to see that she knew that's the way I like them to look.

I rushed back to the storage room and looked around for the book, but nothing was there. With so much on my mind, I was sure it had to be at home.

I gave one more look behind the counter before I noticed my cauldron was empty.

"A..." My heart raced. I felt faint. "Faith, did you mess with my cauldron while I was in the back?" I prayed she didn't think it was dirty and cleaned it.

"No. I'm not that stupid." She flipped the sign to open.

Frantically, I ran all over the shop looking for any signs of the potion. It wasn't like it grew legs and walked away.

There was a rush of butterflies to my gut. Something or someone had taken my potion, which meant they took the book. My first instinct was to get the police. That wasn't going to happen. The two things that were missing were the two things I had done illegally.

The bell over the door chimed when someone came in.

"Good morning!" Eloise swept across the floor. She had on a blue cloak with beading all over the seams. "I'm excited to be starting our new book club."

"I completely forgot." I threw my palm to my forehead. My head hadn't been screwed on lately with all the crazy commotion of the murder, Oscar, and now a break-in. "Faith are you okay without me?"

"Of course." Faith had put an apron on and was behind the counter waiting anxiously for the first customer to come in. "I'm so grateful."

The spark that used to be in her eyes was starting to come back. With a little luck, I would head over to the police station to ask Gandolf about the Gazette before Eloise and I went to Ever After Books.

"What was that about?" Eloise stopped me at A Charming Cure gate.

"I hired Faith to help me out for awhile. It will help both of us out." I pointed across the street. "Before we go to the bookstore, can we go see Gandolf?"

We had to dodge a few tourists on our way over to the station, but stopped to see what everyone was gawking at outside of Glorybee Pet Shop. Petunia was sitting in a chair outside of an animal pen with her arms folded across her body. The scowl on her face was almost as crooked as the hair on her head. She was disheveled from top to bottom. Even the buttons on her shirt were mismatched.

"What is going on?" I tried to be as polite as I could, but seeing her this way was not the normal happy-go-lucky pet shop owner who loved animals that I knew.

"Those animals have to go!" She pointed behind her. All of the animals in the pen were the stray ones. "Last night I heard the most awful commotion coming from the shop. I went in and these animals were biting, scratching, and chasing my sweet animals. They went crazy! Berserk I tell you!"

We stood far away from the pen. The animals gnashed their teeth and threw themselves up against the fence. I wanted to ask Petunia if she believed what Gerald had said he told her about the animals, but decided this wasn't the time or place.

"What is going on?" Eloise, who rarely comes out during the day, had a frightful look in her emerald green eyes.

"Watch out!" A scream from down the street followed by a honking horn caught our attention. Tourists scattered as Patience Karima rode on the ostrich's back as though she were sidesaddle on a horse. Constance Karima was right behind in the pink hearse beeping the horn and screaming for the ostrich to stop.

The ostrich zipped right past us with Patience holding on for dear life and Constance on their tails.

"See!" Petunia pointed and shouted, "Berserk!"

"This is not good." Whispering Falls tugged at my gut. Something was off, way off. Good thing I was on my way to see Gandolf. Maybe he had some answers.

"I'll be back." I assured Petunia before I ran across the street with Eloise and burst into the police station.

Gandolf was the only one in the station. Colton was nowhere to be seen.

"Good morning, June." He stood up and took off his hat. He nodded. "Eloise."

"Really? You think it's a good morning?" I was ticked off and unable to hold my tongue. "First you tell Faith that the Gazette is the first business to be cut from the budget because we have to beef up the police department. Second, the stray animals have all gone crazy. You are telling me that is a good morning?"

"Settle down." He pushed the palms of his hands to the ground like I was a ten-year old.

"Settle down?" I was about to go as berserk as the animals. "You are the sheriff interim. You do not make the rules nor do you know the status of budget cuts. Do your job of finding the person who killed Alexelrod and find out where these animals go," I demanded.

"If you have a problem with my job description, I suggest you see Isadora Solstice." He put his hat back on his head. His eyes bore through me. "If you don't mind, I need to get back to a murder investigation."

He sat back down, picked up his pencil and started flipping through some papers.

"Be expecting me to come back," I growled, assuring him that the way he treated me was not acceptable.

Eloise and I stormed out of the station. One thing was for sure, Gandolf was going to be replaced by Colton, and fast.

"Who exactly did he think he was talking to?" I stomped down the street, passing by Ever After Books.

"Calm down." Eloise was always the voice of reason. Today was not a day to be reasoned with. I was mad and I was going to get to the bottom of this. Whispering Falls was falling apart and it wasn't going to continue under my administration.

"Is she in there?" Eloise asked when we got to Mystic Lights and the sign was still turned to closed.

We planted our faces up against the windows and looked in. The lights were out. Izzy had been sick due to some crazy issues a few months ago, so I chalked up her not being there due to her still recovering.

"I will check on her later." Eloise said as we made our way back to Ever After Books.

"Let me know how she is. She looked good at the meeting before everything crumbled," I said, referring to Alexelrod's murder. Eloise and Izzy had been friends for a long time. "Don't tell her what is going on around here. It can wait until she's feeling better."

"I will." Eloise kept her lips tight. Though she was my mom's best friend and much older than me, she respected my place in the community. She knew when to give advice and knew when not to.

"What do you say we head on in?" I couldn't wait for Eloise to see the inside of Ever After Books. It was the most spectacular bookstore I had ever seen. I pointed out the colorful daisies and beautifully and oddly shaped bushes. Seeing them reminded me of the spell book, who took it, and my potion. The only person I could tell all of this to was no longer someone I could confide in...Oscar.

If he were still a spiritualist, I'd be able to tell him everything, and he'd help find out who did it.

The bookstore was packed. Aisle upon aisle of customers browsed the shelves and were putting books in their hand-held baskets. All of the tables were full as well as the cute loveseats that were positioned all over the store.

Ever After Books had to be the most popular shop in Whispering Falls. Raven Mortimer even had a bakery stand in the back corner where her pre-made baked goodies sat in single-serve bags.

"Wow." Eloise racked at the edges of her short red hair. She stood with her mouth open in awe of all the stuff going on.

Ophelia had several employees helping customers and some were helping children doing crafts in the children's section.

"Good morning, ladies." Ophelia welcomed us with open arms. Her long curly honey-blond hair hung down her back. She wore a long black skirt with a bright blue sleeveless top. "What can I help you find today?"

"We were wanting to start a book club." Eloise picked a book off the shelf before replacing it.

"How can I help you?" Ophelia asked again as if she didn't hear Eloise.

"We want you to recommend a book for our new book club." Eloise stated her request a little differently this time.

"Are you here to look around?" Ophelia's eyes wandered from shelf to shelf, pulling books in and out as she went.

I put my hand on her arm to stop her. She looked at me with a scowl.

"Are you okay?" I questioned her.

"No." She grabbed my hand and dragged me to the back of the shop. I hoped she wasn't going to ask me to do the same crazy follow me stunt she pulled the other night. She didn't. Once Eloise and I were in the back office, Ophelia shut the door.

"I've misplaced something of the utmost importance." Her voice was even more high-pitched when she was nervous. "It's a book of spells, and if it gets into the wrong hands, we are all in trouble."

"That wasn't the book I wanted for book club." Eloise was uncomfortable with any sort of spell. She'd rather stay in her treehouse deep in the woods than come to Whispering Falls. "We don't know where your book is. Let's go, June." Eloise tugged at my shirtsleeve.

"Hold on." I pulled away. "Was it 'Mysteries and Magical Spells?'"

"Yes! Do you know where it is?" She asked urgently, almost pleading.

"I did." I stopped and took a breath. "Then someone stole it."

"What?" Eloise and Ophelia cried out in unison.

"The day Alexelrod was found, it was outside under a bush. I picked it up and took it back to my shop where I put it behind the counter." I shuffled my feet. They were not going to like the last part I was about to tell them.

"Unfortunately, last night someone broke into my shop and stole a potion I was making, and the book is gone."

"Oh no." Ophelia looked more like a frightened child in a witch costume rather than a real witch. "I'm afraid we are in more trouble than you realize."

A lump sat in my throat. My stomach was doing summersaults. There was no denying it. My intuition was in full swing. Whispering Falls was in trouble and it was up to me to get us out of this mess.

Chapter Twenty

My day wasn't getting any better. In fact it was getting worse. The animals were acting crazier than ever, Constance couldn't find Patience, who was still hanging on to and riding the ostrich because she refused to let him run off, and the "Mysteries and Magical Spells" book was missing.

I had searched A Charming Cure high and low for any sign of a break-in, only to come up empty handed. I even walked back to my cottage to see if I had put it there and to figure out if the potion had evaporated. Nothing.

The knock on the cottage door stopped me from almost taking a knife to the couch cushions because I was so desperate.

"Colton?" Of all people to show up. While standing on the front porch, I wondered if my crazed appearance in the shadow of the sun would make any man run for the woods. I raked my fingers through my hair, and then swiped under my eyes. I was a sweaty mess and I was sure my mascara was halfway down my face by now. "Come in."

"Are you okay?" His looked all buff in his gold-rimmed Ray Ban sunglasses and Whispering Falls uniform.

"I'm a little out of sorts." I was reluctant to tell him why. The way I saw it, I was in a pickle and had no choice. He was as close to Oscar would be in helping me, only not in the romantic department, though he *was* pleasant to look at. "You are going to think I'm a crazy Village President that doesn't know what she's doing."

"Ya think?" He half-grinned, teasing me.

"Whatever." I smacked his arm. He followed me to the couch and we sat down. "Anyway, I found this book at the scene of the crime and picked it up. I didn't think it had anything to do with Alexelrod's murder before, but now I think I'm wrong. I think it had a lot to do with the murder, but I'm not sure what."

"What kind of book?" Colton sat back and his shirt tugged a little tighter around his chest.

"You aren't going to tell Gandolf are you?" I wanted to make sure he kept Gandolf out of the loop, because I was going to get Gandolf out of the picture as soon as I talked to Izzy.

"He is so busy with the budget cut that he isn't even looking at other suspects." Colton's distaste for how Gandolf was running the investigation was apparent.

"It's a 'Mysteries and Magical Spells' book that Ophelia kept at the shop. I picked it up because of O..." I almost slipped and said Oscar. That was a situation that Colton didn't need to know about. It had nothing to do with the murder. Oscar's dilemma was my fault, my problem. I shook it off. "...I was curious and left it at A Charming Cure along with a special potion I'm making. When I went to work today, the potion and the book were gone."

"June, what kind of potion?" He seemed as if he was almost afraid to ask.

"A power potion," I mumbled. Colton was not going to like that in the slightest bit. I covered my mouth and said, "An enhanced power potion."

"June!" He sucked in a deep breath; his shirt became even more snug, showing off those muscles under the shirt. "We will deal with the potion later. What about the book?"

"When I confessed to Ophelia that I took the book and it was missing, she said that there were some ancient potions in there and that if they fell into the wrong hands, we were in deep trouble." I pointed to my gut. "And I feel like it has already gotten into the wrong hands along with my potion."

Colton got up and paced the length of the couch, scratching his head like his fingers were going to give him some good ideas.

"I think that Alexelrod didn't go to the meeting that night because he thought everyone would be there. He slipped into Ever After and took the book. Then whoever wanted the book, was in there too and found the dart book. They shot him with the darts on his way out and that is when Faith saw him. The killer ran off after Faith started to scream."

Colton stopped dead in his tracks, his eyes narrowed. "You have this all figured out."

I sat up a little taller with a big smile on my face. I had completely just solved the crime. I was pleased as a plum.

"So who killed him?" Colton's question deflated my oversized ego.

"I don't know." I slumped back into the cushions of the couch. "Good question."

"Which brings us back to Ophelia Biblio." His voice drifted off. "Do you think she did it?"

"I don't. And I don't necessarily know if the person meant to kill anyone, but did because Alexelrod was in the way." I had played the scenario in my head so many times everything was getting foggy. "The person had to know that there was a meeting that night."

"Ophelia, Alexelrod, and Faith were the only ones not there." Colton brought us back to the only two suspects and victim. "Only Faith checked out on her alibi and Ophelia hasn't."

"There has to be something we are missing, besides the book." That book was the key to this entire piece. "Whoever has the book is the killer."

There was no way around it. Once those words left my mouth, my intuition kicked in and I knew better than ever that I had to find the "Mysteries and Magical Spells" book.

"In the meantime, I've got to go see Izzy and get Gandolf taken off the case. It's time you took over as the new Sheriff of Whispering Falls." There was no need to tell Colton about Faith and the budget cuts or her working for me. That sort of complicated matters didn't concern him, only me as the Village President. "As the president," I decided to pull rank, "I want you to work on the leads of finding the potion and the book. Do not mention any of this to Gandolf."

"Oh, I won't." He put his sunglasses back on his face and headed out the door.

"Oh please," Madame Torres's voice dripped out from my bag. "Stop staring at his tush and ask him out."

"Nope! I have Oscar…or…I *will* have Oscar." I glanced at the time. It was almost time for me to drive to Locust Grove for dinner at Oscar's house.

Chapter Twenty-One

"You are staying here tonight," I said to Mr. Prince Charming who was sitting on my dresser. He knew that I was going somewhere and I was going without him. It was high time I had some alone time with Oscar, and I mean alone. No cat, no crystal ball just Oscar and me.

The purple dress went perfectly with my black hair. I was even pleased with the way my hair turned out. I even put on my purple strappy sandals. If Oscar didn't notice me in this outfit, then he was blind.

"I'm out of here!" I grabbed my bag and took Madame Torres out. "You are staying here."

"Did you check out your Make-Me-A-Match profile yet?" Madame Torres asked.

"Don't need it. I have Oscar." I put her on the counter and grabbed the keys to the Green Machine, my old green El Camino.

"Don't be so sure." I ignored her comment, refusing to let her put doubt in my head and ruin my night.

I made sure the door was locked. Suddenly I felt sick. Someone had to have known I had the "Mysteries and Magical Spells" book if they broke into A Charming Cure to steal it. What would I do if they tried to break into my house?

I jumped into the Green Machine and gave her a good pat on the dashboard. "Okay, girl. Let's go back to Locust Grove, but we have to stop at the police station first."

It wasn't like my car could hear me, but I still treated her like one of the family. I eased the El Camino out onto Main Street with my eyes peeled out for Colton. He was standing next to Gandolf in front of Ever After Books, in the exact same spot where Faith had found Alexelrod.

I pulled over and when Colton looked my way, I waved him over.

"Where are you headed?" He stuck his head in the passenger window. He let out a little whistle when he saw my dress and raised his eyebrows.

"Out with a friend."

"It must be a *special* friend," he said.

"Listen, I need you to do me a favor." I looked over his shoulder and noticed Gandolf staring at us. "I don't want anyone to know, but I'm going to Locust Grove for a few hours. Can you keep an eye on my house?"

"Sure, but what are you doing in Locust Grove?" His voice was stern.

"I told you, I'm going out with my boy..." I stopped myself. "My old boyfriend."

"Lucky guy." He smiled and pulled back. His hands gripped the side of the door with his arms extended out. "I'll be sure to watch out for you."

"Great." I shifted the Green Machine into drive, waved bye and headed out of town.

It had been so long since I had driven to Locust Grove, I had almost forgotten how pretty the drive was. Maybe it just was the fantastic mood I was in.

Leaving the spiritual world behind, I turned my radio up, rolled my windows down and sang at the top of my lungs. This was going to be a great night.

Chapter Twenty-Two

"Here goes everything." I looked in the rearview mirror and patted down my windblown hair. With a little dab of lipstick, I was ready to go.

I felt a little ping of sadness when I looked over at the small house across the street from Oscar's where I grew up. There were so many memories of Darla and Oscar. The house had long since been replaced with another family. Oscar had said they were good people. And Mac McGurtle's place next door was also taken over by a new family.

I snickered when I noticed that the charred remains of the shed I had burned down were still in a pile at the side of the house.

"You look great." Oscar stood at his door with a big grin on his face. He had on a pair of blue jeans, and the white v-neck tee looked great against his tanned skin and black hair. My heart skipped a beat. I did have on the perfect outfit for the perfect night.

"Nothing but the best for my bestest friend." I sashayed up to the house, making sure that I didn't fall down and make a complete joke of myself in these heels.

"Great to see you." He grabbed me and gave me a bear hug. I started to return the favor when I looked over his shoulder and saw another woman.

Her long brown hair tumbled past her breasts and her legs were a mile long in her blue jean mini romper. Her toenails were a perfect red and were slid into cute blue and khaki wedge heels.

"I didn't know you had company." I didn't take my eyes off her. She was smiling so big that I felt like smacking the grin off of her face but then thought maybe it was someone who worked with Oscar that didn't realize I was his girlfriend and was coming over...*was his girlfriend* was the phrase that didn't sit well with me.

"I couldn't wait for you two to meet." Oscar reached out and I went to grab his hand, but he locked hands with *hers*.

Instantly, the room began to spin and there was complete darkness.

"Is she okay?" The woman's voice, which I didn't recognize, asked.

"She's fine." The sweet sounds of Oscar's voice filled my ears and I remembered where I was and what had happened. "She does this all the time."

"I should really check her out." I felt the woman's finger on my neck and I jerked up.

I must have startled her when I jumped up, because she flung herself back but Oscar caught her fall and they laughed.

"Are you okay?" Oscar's attention was totally on her and not me. He had always made sure I was okay after passing out before, but not this time.

My eyes narrowed as I zeroed in on her. She was everything I was not; feminine, and in Oscar's arms.

"Tend to her." She smiled, pulled away from Oscar and brushed her hands down the front of her outfit.

It was as if slow motion had taken over my world. Oscar kissed her. On. The. Lips. She didn't smack him or pull away.

My mouth dropped. Everything went black again.

Chapter Twenty-Three

"How could he do this to me?" I screamed, questioning what had happened a few hours earlier once I had come to and realized my worst nightmares had come true.

Oscar didn't love me. More importantly, he had a girlfriend.

"How did this happen?" My head was buried in my stack of pillows on my bed. I had put Madame Torres on my nightstand when I got home. I was desperate if I wanted her company. I flung a pillow off my face. I eyed Madame Torres. "Did you know about this?"

"I told you not to expect anything." She did seem to be loving the fact that she was always right. "And I told you to check out Make-Me-A-Match to see who responded to your profile."

"I'm not interested in anyone but Oscar." I buried the pillow back over my face and sobbed. There was no way that I had spent all my life trying to get Oscar to love me and lose him to some, some...ugh! I hated that she was nice.

"She... she..." I didn't even recall her name. "She can't be that nice."

The knock at the door caused me to jump up. I was sure it was Colton since I asked him to keep an eye on my house. I had forgotten all about the intruder and deep down wished the intruder would break in and put me out of my misery.

I opened the door with Mr. Prince Charming standing next to me.

"Oscar?"

"Have you been crying?" *Now* he had a look of concern on his face. He stepped inside and put his hands on my arms. "Are you okay, June? You have been passing out a lot lately. Maybe Annie can take a look at you."

"Annie? Her name is Annie?" I rolled my eyes and jerked away. "What is *Annie* going to do for me?"

"She's a doctor." Oscar stayed on the threshold watching me pace like some crazy cat. I pounded my head with my hand trying to get the image of *Annie* and Oscar kissing out of it.

Hiss, hiss. Mr. Prince Charming darted back down the hall when he saw Oscar.

"She can't fix me!" I stomped my feet. "She needs to fix you!"

"June, you need to calm down."

"I need to calm down?" I blurted through my tears. "You need to calm down and realize you are a sorcerer!"

He jerked back and folded his arms.

"Yea, a sorcerer! Like in magic!" I waved my hands around like I was doing some sort of spell. "We…" I gestured between the two of us, "are spiritualists. Your parents and my dad did some bat-crazy magic and I'm a real homeopathic Curist with intuitive skills. I know what people need and you don't need *Annie!*"

He continued to look at me as if I was a couple of cups of crazy.

I continued to spill the beans.

"You and I moved here and you were the sheriff before you decided to go to the Order of Elders and denounce your heritage because we were in *love* and you wanted to save me from going to jail!" I pointed between us. "*We* were in love. A couple. An item!"

"Calm down." He patted his hands toward the ground. "I really do think we need to go to the hospital."

"I don't need a hospital, Oscar." The tears were pouring down my face. "I'm the Village President here! I

went to a special spiritualist school! Eloise is your aunt!
You do not like Annie!"

"You have gone crazy." Oscar shook his head. "I told
you not to move to this village. I begged you, but you did it
anyway."

He turned and walked out the door.

I stomped after him.

"Where do you think you are going?" I screamed at
him in the dead night air.

"I'm getting out of this crazy village and going home."
He stopped next to his car and turned around. "Good bye,
June. And for the record, I do love Annie!"

He got in his car and slammed the door. Never once
did his break lights come on.

Chapter Twenty-Four

"Hello?" I grabbed my cell off my nightstand before I even looked to see who it was or even the time. When Oscar left, I threw myself back under the covers wishing that I was next on the killer's list. I even left my door unlocked, hoping to be the next victim.

"Are you coming to work today?" Faith asked on the other end of the line.

"What time is it?" I kept my eyes shut. My stomach sank when I realized I was still breathing. The killer didn't want me either.

"It's past ten am." There was some noise in the background. "I'm here and have opened the shop. You had a line of customers waiting at the door. What do you want me to do?"

"I'm taking the day off." I shut the phone off and put it back on my nightstand. I didn't have the energy to help people when I couldn't even help myself.

Ophelia! I threw back the covers and threw on some sweatpants. There was one person that could help me. Ophelia Biblio.

"Let's go." I grabbed Madame Torres and my bag before I bolted out the door and down the hill.

The sun was so bright, like it was mocking me. Why couldn't it have rained? At least that would have fit my mood. There was a line outside of A Charming Cure and I didn't dare go in. I was in no mood to help other people. I had to help Oscar see that he was making a big mistake with *Annie*.

Her name made me want to throw up. "She's a doctor," I mocked him in my best voice.

"Who is a doctor?"

"Oh!" I stopped before I realized I was at the steps of Ever After Books. Ophelia was on her knees in the colorful daisy bed with her gardening bucket next to her. "Can't you just twirl your finger and make them grow?" I questioned her witching abilities. If she couldn't grow daisies with her magic, she certainly wasn't going to be able to help me.

"I could, but I enjoy being out here and doing normal things." She stood up and took off her gloves. "Who is a doctor? You look like you need to see one."

Her eyes scanned up and down, taking in a good look of what crazy looked like. Me.

I looked around, making sure no one was listening to us, but you never knew in this place. "I need your help in a way that can never be spoken of again."

"Why don't we go inside?" She suggested in her high-pitched voice and led the way up the stairs and through the bookstore to her office in the back.

She shut the door once I was in. "Have a seat."

I let out a sigh of relief once I sat down. I was exhausted mentally and physically. The mirror on her wall confirmed it when I barely recognized myself. My eyes were red and swollen. My lips were bright red and chapped from my chewing on them.

"I look awful." I noted. "And for good reasons."

"What might those be?" Ophelia smiled, giving me a warm fuzzy feeling. I let her in on how I needed her help.

"I need you to put a spell on Dr. Annie."

"A spell?"

"Yep. One certified ugly witch spell." That should cover it.

"I'm a Good-Sider. I don't do ugly witch spells." She leaned up against her desk and folded her hands in front of her. "Who is Dr. Annie and why do we want to put an ugly spell on her?"

"Because she stole Oscar from me." There wasn't much more to it than that. Well, maybe a little more. Ophelia wasn't buying it. "Okay…" I paused before I led into the big spill about what had happened with Oscar from my past to the present. "So will you put an ugly spell on her?"

"That is a lot to swallow." Ophelia didn't agree to do any sort of spell on Annie. "I can't put a spell on her, but we can have some fun at her expense."

"Really?" I rubbed my hands together. "Like what?" I was anxious to hear.

"You meet me here tonight around…" she tapped her wristwatch, "around seven. Leave all the work to me."

"Deal." I stuck my hand out for her to shake on it.

She crinkled her nose and shook her head. "Just get a shower and clean up."

With a plan in place, I left the office. Eloise, Petunia and Raven were sitting in a circle in one of the reading areas of the bookstore. Each of them had a copy of the book "Gone With The Ghost" in their hands.

"Hey, guys." I greeted them and sat next to Raven. "Did you start the book club without me?"

Dang. First Oscar disses me, now my friends.

"No." Eloise tilted her head and gave me a strange look. "We all just happened to be in here at the same time."

"I was filling up my little free-standing baked goods display over there." There was pride on Raven's face. "Who knew that readers love their brownies and cupcakes as much as they love their books?"

"I had to get away from those crazy animals." Petunia still looked a little discombobulated. "I'm about to go off my rocker."

"They still aren't talking to you?" It was so odd. I had never seen animals react to Petunia any other way than with love. Those animals were not into love what-so-ever.

"No." There was a deep-set sadness in her eyes. The hurt ran through her entire body and my intuition could feel it.

"What is wrong with you? You are all..." Eloise brought a cautious eye.

"I guess I should tell you since you think I'm going crazy." For about a split second, I wasn't going to tell them, but I couldn't keep it bottled up any longer. "Oscar has a girlfriend."

They all gasped.

"Turned out my dinner for two, was dinner for three." I pointed to myself. "I ended up being the third wheel."

Eloise closed her eyes. Her chest heaved up and down. I put my hand on her leg.

"Are you okay?" I asked, but knew the answer. It devastated her as much as it did me. There was always a hope that one day Oscar and I would have a family of our own, and our children would call Eloise their aunt.

"We will always know the truth and his love runs so deep for you that he altered his life forever." Eloise had the ability to always see the bright side, even as a Dark-Sider.

"I call crap on that," Raven said it like it was. "You have a right to be mad. He'll be back." Raven nodded.

"It doesn't end there." I went on to tell them how I let him in on the little spiritual secret and how he ran off like wasps were chasing him. "He couldn't get out of Whispering Falls fast enough."

"I wish he would have taken some of those animals with him on his way out." Petunia stood up. She was never great in the love department. She and Gerald kept their affair on the QT even though everyone in town knew about it. "Speaking of animals, Oscar included, I have to get back. I'll start on the book. When do you guys want to meet?"

"I'll figure out a date and we can have tea at my house." Eloise graciously offered her house for the book club meetings, which was fine with me. My house was still a disaster from me tearing it up looking for the spell book.

"I have to get going too." Raven stood up and held the book close to her. "June, come on by and I'll send some Gems home with you."

"Sounds great." I smiled. This little pity-party was turning out in my favor. Now there was only Eloise to deal with. I knew she was going to give me an earful exactly the way Darla would have. I turned toward her and held my hands out. "Go on. Scold me."

"I'm not going to scold you." She gave me a sympathy look. "You have been through enough. I just hope the Elders don't find out or you will be in trouble for telling him."

"I never thought about that." In the heat of the moment I was so mad at him that I didn't care what he heard.

"I hope you understand that it isn't his fault." Although Eloise tried to make me feel better, it only made me feel worse.

"I know." There wasn't one second that went by that I didn't blame myself. "I did this to him, you and me."

"Are you two okay over here?" Ophelia turned the corner. She shuffled a couple of books on the shelves around and straightened a few more.

"We have gotten everything we need to start our book club." Eloise held up the copy of "Gone With The Ghost."

"Classic." Ophelia tapped the cover. "A perfect pick for your first read."

"I'll see you two later." Eloise held the book to her chest. "June, don't you worry. Everything is going to turn out exactly the way it should."

Ophelia and I watched Eloise walk up to the cashier. There was a line ten people deep.

"The bookstore is a hit." I was glad to see that business wasn't affected by the recent turn of events. I stepped back and couldn't help but wonder if Ophelia had anything to do with Alexelrod. I took the stand on innocent until proven guilty, but all the evidence did point to her.

"I'm very pleased." She averted her attention to me. "I can't wait until tonight." She winked before she turned to go back to work.

There was still my little issue with Izzy. Why had she had hired a new sheriff without telling me? It was not that I doubted her; after all, she'd been the Village President for years and knew what she was doing. But it was odd that she hadn't consulted me.

Chapter Twenty-Five

The glass windows of Mystic Lights did confirm what Ophelia had told me. I needed to get cleaned up. The reflection of my hair sticking up all over the place and my frumpy clothes didn't look like the image of a good leader. I wasn't feeling anywhere near to leading anyone except Annie. I would gladly lead her out of Oscar's heart.

I tapped on Mystic Lights door after reading the closed sign and jiggled the locked handle. Izzy would never be closed this long unless she was very sick or something was very wrong.

A Charming Cure was fine with Faith running it and it was a much needed break for me to go see Aunt Helena at Hidden Hall A Spiritualist University and visit Wands, Potions, and Beyond. My cauldron had to be replaced and fast. If Ophelia was going to work her witchy way to help me get rid of Annie, Oscar was sure to come running back into my arms and I was going to have the potion all ready for him.

"There you are." Mr. Prince Charming darted in front of me as we made our way up the hill toward the path that leads to Hidden Hall. We came to the wheat field where there was a sign in the middle of nowhere that no one but a spiritualist could see.

I tapped the sign and several wooden arms that pointed in several different directions popped out. I looked for the one that had Hidden Hall A Spiritualist University written on it and touched it. As always, like magic, the wheat field parted and a stone walkway made a nice path for Mr. Prince Charming and me to follow.

I smiled at the small yellow cottage that had window boxes under each window that overflowing with Geraniums, Morning Glories, Petunias, Moon Flowers, and

Trailing Ivy, leaving a rainbow of colorful explosion. The awning flapping in the light breeze read "Intuition School" in lime green calligraphy and made me smile as I thought back to my first day of intuition school.

We passed the cottage and made our way into the college town. All of the fun hangouts were overflowing with college students.

"Hello, June Heal." The male voice spoke softly in my ear.

Gus Chatham didn't have to be present for me to know it was him. Gus was a medium who also had the cool powers of Teletransporting. He liked to freak people out with his on the fly comments in people's ears without them seeing him.

"Good afternoon, Gus." I patted my hair down. It was probably a good idea that I had cleaned myself up before I came to Hidden Hall, and from all the crazy stares, I still didn't look normal.

Gus appeared, walking next to me. He looked as great as ever with his shaggy surfer-dude, ash-blond hair. Tall and lanky, his cargo pants still hung past the waist of his underwear.

"What do we owe the pleasure?" Gus asked. He was Aunt Helena's right hand guy. People referred to him as *the eyes and ears of the dean*. I'd call him a tattletale. "Helena didn't say to expect you."

"I didn't tell her I was coming." I pointed toward Wands, Potions, and Beyond. "My cauldron broke and I need a new one."

I left out the little part about how it broke with me doing an illegal potion, in fear he'd tell Aunt Helena, who had considered herself my mother since Darla passed away.

"Let me go get her."

Before I could tell him not to bother her yet, he was gone. Any minute I was sure a puff of smoke would appear and Aunt Helena would be standing in the middle. She always loved to make a grand entrance. I made it inside of Wands, Potions, and Beyond without the slightest sign of smoke.

"Good afternoon." The clerk waved from behind the counter. "Is there anything I can help you find?"

Even though I had been in the store several times, I stood there with my mouth open taking in all it had to offer. Floors upon floors of wands, potions, ingredients, how-to books, cauldrons, cloaks, food, clothes, and anything else a spiritualist would need.

"I'm looking to buy a new cauldron." I smiled and pointed up to the one hundred and twentieth floor where I knew the large ones were located. There was even a dash of smoke coming from that floor over the staircase railing from all the display cauldrons.

"I'll get your ride." The clerk picked up a phone. "Customer needing to go to floor 120," her voice said over the intercom.

Within seconds there was a young sorcerer assisting me to the elevator and escorting me to the cauldrons.

"Take your time and push the button when you are ready." He pointed to the pole near the elevator that was marked for assistance.

"Thanks." I smiled and took in row upon row of cauldrons. They have come a long way from the black ones from long ago or even the plastic cauldrons we used at Halloween when I was a child.

They came in all shapes and sizes. There was even a tricked-out one with sparkly bling wrapped in pictures. I made it over to the regular aisle, the cheaper ones. I wanted one exactly like the one I had before. I knew how it worked and didn't have time to even think about learning how to use a new one.

"It's about time you upgraded." Aunt Helena turned the corner with her arms wide open – her signature black cloak swinging with each step. Her long fingers with long red fingernails curled around me, squeezing me tight.

"It's so good to see you." I hugged her back. There was something so comforting knowing that I wasn't alone in the world. "I'm not here to upgrade. I want a new one just like the one I had." I pointed to the same exact one.

Aunt Helena clapped. The cauldron disappeared.

"Done." She brushed her hands together. "It's in your shop now."

"Thanks." I was glad to know that I didn't have to pay any shipping or handling or haul it back by myself.

"Let's have lunch." Her brows and lips lifted into a smile. I didn't have time to protest before her pointy red boots clicked along the store tile and made our way to the elevator where the customer service sorcerer was already waiting for us.

He bowed when he saw Aunt Helena and she nodded back so he could stand up.

"I'm sorry I had no idea you were June Heal, the dean's niece." There was more fright in his eyes than his shaky voice.

I shooed my hands in the air. "No big deal. Really. I'm a big girl."

"I'm so glad you are here." Aunt Helena and I made our way out of the shop and on to the street. I could feel Gus around us without seeing that he was there, secretly floating next to us. "How long are you staying?"

"Just for a quick lunch, then I have to get back to the shop." I didn't know if I should ask her now for a potion or what. So I decided to wait until we were seated at the Black

Magic Café, a deliciously wonderful little café on the edge
of campus that served anything you wanted.

Raven Mortimer had worked there while she was in
college.

"I'll have the crow burger with eye-of-newt bun." Aunt
Helena told the waitress who was still in a full-blown bow
before she was given the *get up* nod.

"I'll have the same." It was so much easier to order
two instead of taking time to look at the menu. I glanced
down at my watch and noticed it was already four o'clock.
The time flew by, leaving me little time to get back to
Whispering Falls to work on Oscar's potion, find Izzy, and
meet Ophelia at seven.

During our lunch I told Aunt Helena about the potion.
She already knew about Oscar, and I waited to see what she
had to say.

"You need to leave it alone," She warned. "Let nature
take its course just like your mother and father."

"You're kidding, right?" I was a bit confused. Aunt
Helena loved a good potion and loved testing them out on
different subjects.

"No." She drew in a breath before she snapped her
fingers and disappeared before my eyes.

"I guess that is a no," I whispered and picked up my
cup to take a sip.

"But I can help." The ever-so-devious Gus appeared
next to me in Aunt Helena's seat. "I've been dying around
here, I'm so bored."

The look in his eye was deep, holding onto a secret
that I couldn't wait to see unfold.

Chapter Twenty-Six

With a little bit of planning with Gus underway, I headed back to Whispering Falls. Mr. Prince Charming darted in and out of the wheat field, swaying his tail in sync with the wheat.

There was no time to worry about going back to the shop. Ophelia had told me to clean up and I had just enough time to do that before I met her.

"There you are." Colton sat on the step of my front porch when we walked up. "I've been looking all over for you."

"Oh." I pulled out my key and opened the door.

Rowl! Mr. Prince Charming darted off the porch and headed down the hill.

The inside of the cottage looked like a tornado had hit. The kitchen table and chairs were overturned, as well as the couch.

"Oh no." We stepped over broken picture frames to get inside. Everything that I owned lay strewn all over the floor. In the corner of the room, there was a faint glow. "Madame Torres!"

I almost broke a leg getting to her. The globe pulsed slowly, like she was starving for air. There was a small crack in the glass from being thrown.

"No!" I screamed. "No!"

"What's wrong?" Colton rushed over and bent down next to me.

"It's my crystal ball. She's barely hanging on to life." I snuggled her close to me, wondering what I was going to do to help her. I felt an acute sense of loss. "They win!"

"No, June, they don't." Colton rushed around the cottage with his gun drawn searching to make sure the intruder was gone. "They will not destroy our village."

"I will help." A faint whisper appeared in my ear. It was Gus. "Shh…don't tell him I'm here. Leave Madame Torres near the Gathering Rock when you leave to meet Ophelia."

I didn't even nod. If Gus didn't want Colton to know, then he wouldn't know. I had to save my friend and nothing was going to stop me. I was going to find this killer before they destroyed us.

Chapter Twenty-Seven

Colton had to get Gandolf involved, which was fine since he was the acting sheriff. When I asked Gandolf if he had seen Izzy, he said he hadn't because he was too busy creating a case against Ophelia. I could see Colton snarl. Colton definitely didn't like Gandolf's old-school ways.

"What's going on?" Ophelia stepped into the cottage and quickly withdrew when she saw Gandolf and Colton. My intuition told me that they made her uncomfortable; at least Gandolf did.

Gandolf looked at the door where Ophelia had been and then back to me. He pulled out his little notebook and wrote something down.

It was a few more minutes before the two men collected some fingerprints and other things they deemed as evidence of the break-in, and then they left.

Once they were safely at a distance, Ophelia reappeared. My mood sharply turned from fear to anger as I told Ophelia about what had happened to my cottage and Madame Torres. My soul seethed with mounting anger. There was no gut feeling telling me she had anything to do with it. I quickly found some clothes to wear out of the mess that had been strewn all over the floor from the intruder dumping my drawers out.

"Let's go." Ophelia waved her hand in the air and before I knew it, we were seated in a restaurant right behind Oscar and Annie, only they couldn't see us. I glared at Annie's perfect bun she had pinned up on her pretty head. I cringed, knowing she'd be pretty even if she were bald.

"There they are." I pointed to them.

"I know." A devious smile crept up on Ophelia's face and she pointed to Annie right as Annie was taking sip of wine.

Instantly, the wine glass tipped, sending dribbles down Annie's chin and landing on her white eyelet dress leaving a waterfall of red wine stain.

"Oh my," Annie squealed.

Like the good gentleman he was, Oscar stood up and dabbed Annie with his napkin and they laughed it off.

As Annie laughed, a pair of dentures flew out of her mouth. Annie's hands juggled them in the air as she tried to catch them, only they landed right in Oscar's mashed potatoes.

My mouth and cheeks puffed out ready to explode as I held in my laughter. It was like watching something from a movie.

Ophelia winked. "The show has just begun." She pointed her finger again. Annie's hair fell out of the bun and off her head. "Extensions." Ophelia giggled.

Annie burst into tears and ran out of the restaurant with Oscar hot on her heels.

"Little miss priss isn't as lovely as she wants everyone to believe." Ophelia snapped her fingers and we were back at my cottage.

"I feel awful." There was a little sadness in my heart, and some guilt sitting in my stomach like a rock. "I don't think we were very nice."

"Oh, who cares about nice?" Ophelia snapped again and she was gone.

"I care!" I shouted, feeling even more doom and gloom. I waited for a moment to see if she was going to respond, but she didn't.

I headed on down to Ever After Books to get a little validation as to why I had asked her to do it. It was sort of like beating a dead horse. I needed to beat that horse to justify why I was breaking Oscar's heart when I should truly be happy for him if he did care about her.

Chapter Twenty-Eight

"You better put me down now!" The voice caught my attention.

There was a glow floating down the hill right behind me.

"I said now you big buffoon!"

I knew that voice. "Madame Torres?" I questioned as the glow got closer.

"Tell him to put me down," she screamed into the night.

Gus appeared to be holding her with both hands. He shoved her toward me. "If I could have strangled her I would have."

I took her in my hands and kissed her crack-free globe all over. *Mwah! Mwah! Mwah!*

"Oh, stop it!" *Blech, blech, blech.* Madame Torres spit.

"Thank you, thank you, thank you!" I threw my arms around Gus and planted a big ole kiss on his cheek. "You are the best. I have to run!"

I darted off in the direction of Ever After Books. Now that I had Madame Torres back, I was happy and I wanted Oscar to be happy. I had to get Ophelia to help me rectify the situation we just caused with Oscar and Annie.

"But I have to tell you about…" I heard Gus shouting into the night.

I couldn't make out what he was saying, but it had to wait. Oscar was my main concern.

"I'll come find you tomorrow!" I screamed back into the night and hugged Madame Torres tight to me.

"She's going to figure it out," I heard a woman whisper as I approached Ever After Books.

"Shh…" Madame Torres warned me to be careful and quiet. I slowly nodded my head and tiptoed around the side of the bookstore.

"I know she's going to figure it out, so let her."

I peeked around the corner and saw Colton talking to Ophelia. They were in a heated discussion about someone.

"We aren't on June's radar." Ophelia confirmed that I was so totally consumed with Oscar that I didn't realize Whispering Falls was crumbling right in front of me, even though I said it wouldn't.

"She could figure it out any minute." Colton warned her.

"So what do you suggest we do? Kill her?" Ophelia had a half-joking, half-not joking grin on her face before Colton grabbed her and laid a kiss on her that she would probably never forget.

I rubbed my neck to loosen the tense muscles.

"Is she going to strangle me?" I asked Madame Torres. I rubbed harder trying to get out the knot that had settled there. The tension traveled to my stomach and then fell all the way to my toes. "Wait."

I brought Madame Torres closer to my face. She stared at me. I didn't like the look in her eyes.

"Are they," I gulped, "the killers?"

Madame Torres swirled and twirled in her globe until she shut off. Everything played in my head. All the times Colton had come to my house, he was probably prepping me. Was he the one who broke into my house? After all, he was the only one who knew I was gone because I was dumb enough to ask him to watch my house.

I had confided in him. I told him everything about the "Mysteries and Magical Spells" book. If he and Ophelia didn't have it, who did? Did Ophelia and Colton believe that I had the book and tear up my house? Did they hurt my sweet...okay, sweet was a far stretch... my *trustworthy* Madame Torres?

Alexelrod.

Did he know something about Ophelia? Enough for her to kill him, or did Colton kill him for trying to tell the truth about Ophelia, or did Alexelrod know something about Colton?

All sorts of scenarios played out in my head. There was only one person who could answer my questions. Isadora Solstice.

It was time to see her, whether she wanted company or not.

With Madame Torres safely under my arm, I tiptoed my way to Mystic Lights where it was dark, except for a faint glow coming from the back of the shop. I jiggled the door handle, but it was locked.

I covered my eyes as though I was shielding the bright moon. I wanted to get a good look inside. There were two lights glowing and they begged me to come in.

I jiggled the handle one more time to confirm it was locked. There was no time to dilly-dally. The only way to get in – rather, break in – would be to go around the back where no one could see me.

I used my hand to wipe off the muck and mess that was plastered on the back window. Using the hard bottom of Madame Torres to break a hole in the glass window on the back door, so I could slip my hand in and unlock the door, caused the entire glass to crash into tiny little pieces.

"That was easy." I unlocked the door, opened it, and stepped over the bulk of the mess with little crackles of glass breaking under my shoes.

"Izzy?" I asked in a husky whisper. "Izzy?"

The glow I had seen from the window was getting brighter as I approached. There were two crystal balls next to each other, one trying to outshine the other. I took Madame Torres from under my arm and sat her on the counter next to them so I could hold each one to get a better look at them.

"Oh no!" Madame Torres threw her head back. Her eyes bulged from her sockets, blood-shot veins ran rampant through her eyeballs. She glowed green. Electricity shot between Madame Torres and the other two globes, connecting them into a triangle.

"I wanted you to know that a new sheriff has been hired and will be announced at June Heal's first village meeting as the newly elected president." One of the globes showed Izzy talking to someone.

Izzy, where are you? I bent down to get a better look. She looked healthy.

The other globe lit up.

"I think I would like to stay on. Especially since those new animals have surfaced." Gandolf stood with his hand planted on his holster.

"We really do appreciate all of your work, but there has already been a new hire from a village in the west." Izzy turned and it showed her leaving the police station.

The globes played like a movie or as though they were having a conversation and Madame Torres controlled the remote.

Izzy appeared in what seemed to be a new conversation.

"Since Colton is here, it's time for you to leave." Izzy stood next to Gandolf's desk.

"I'm going to help him figure out the solutions to the animals and Alexelrod's murder." Gandolf didn't budge.

"No, you are leaving now." Izzy tugged on his arm. Gandolf jerked, sending Izzy to the ground.

"I told you that I wasn't leaving until the murder is solved." He stood over her with his fist shaking in the air. "You won't tell June Heal anything. Do you understand?"

"There is no way Whispering Falls's budget will work out with two sheriff's salaries." Izzy put her arms in the air to shield herself from him. "I said you are leaving!"

"And I told you I wasn't." Gandolf raised back his hand in the air and sent it flying down, hitting Izzy in the face knocking her out cold.

I watched in horror as the ball showed Gandolf in the middle of all sorts of animals. I leaned in. My eyes squinted. I blinked. I blinked harder.

All of the animals that were strays were standing around Gandolf as he gave them a speech.

"I'm going to free your souls!" He stood like a proud soldier leading a battle. "Whispering Falls is an open community. They are weak and have a new Village President coming into office. We will take over and make it a Dark-Sider community! You will be free from the bondage!"

The animals stomped and brayed, throwing their heads in the air with the good news.

The globe acted as though it had changed a channel.

"Is he inside A Charming Cure?" I gasped, bringing my hand to my mouth. I couldn't believe what I was seeing. Gandolf had broken into my shop. He was the one who took the potion and the book. Suddenly it showed him breaking into Glorybee and feeding the strays the potion.

No wonder they were acting crazy. They took the power potion and couldn't handle it since their bad souls were stuck in the animals and going nuts on poor Petunia.

Petunia. I prayed she was okay, but I had to find out where Gandolf was keeping Izzy.

"Let me go!" Izzy screamed. She looked like she was bound at the feet and her hands were tied behind her back. Gandolf was holding her somewhere, but where?

The next scene showed Gandolf hovered over a woman I didn't recognize. She was stuffing darts with something.

"Poison," Shock and awe ran through me.

"I'm working as fast as I can." The woman sobbed. Gandolf was holding his gun to her side, jabbing it deeper and deeper. She flinched but kept working on the darts.

I tried to get a better look at her, but I didn't recognize her.

I grabbed Madame Torres and threw her under my arm, breaking the connection.

"I've seen enough." I rushed out of the back door and didn't worry about who saw me.

"Gandolf, you think I'm weak," I said through gritted teeth. "I'll show you weak shortly!"

Chapter Twenty-Nine

The streets were dark, but I was sure my anger was shining strong as I stomped my way down to the police station. I didn't know what I was going to do, but I did know that Izzy was somewhere in there. My gut told me so.

The police station door was open as always and I marched right on in. There wasn't a light on and Gandolf wasn't at his desk.

Walking lightly, just in case he was in the building with Izzy and the other woman, I made my way over to his desk. I knew the station well since I had spent a lot of time there with Oscar.

Right on top of the stack of files was Gandolf's application file. I opened it and used Madame Torres as my flashlight.

"Turn the page," Madame Torres coaxed me. "Hurry, June. I don't have a good feeling."

"Now you tell me." I flipped the page and saw an arrest sheet where Gandolf had been stripped of his spiritual powers for killing another spiritualist officer. The statement said that Gandolf claimed he did it out of self-defense but the jury found him guilty.

I ran my finger down the page to see what his punishment was. It said that he not only had been stripped of his duties, but he also had been sentenced to life in prison. A mortal prison.

Right under the punishment there was a big red stamp that said "Wanted." Gandolf was on the run and he was planning on taking over Whispering Falls with the "Mysteries and Magical Spells" book – and he was nearing his goal.

"What do I do?" I asked Madame Torres.

"You should have asked that question before now."
Gandolf stood behind me.

I grimaced when I felt the barrel of a gun jab in my
ribs.

"Come on. Just leave Whispering Falls and I won't tell
anyone anything." I was weak. Being brave was overrated.
"I swear!"

"I don't think so." Gandolf let out a roar of evil
laughter. The deeper he laughed, the deeper the gun went
into my skin. "Walk."

Without a word, I walked forward into the back of the
station where the Sheriff's apartment was. Oscar had lived
there for a short time, so I was a little familiar with it.

Izzy and the other woman were bound and gagged to
the right of the door. Izzy's eyes were deep set with fear.
She dropped her head when she saw it was me.
Disappointment replaced the fright. Instantly, I knew she
had been holding out hope that I would figure out what was
going on.

"Now I'm going to have to kill all three of you."
Gandolf's lip curled on one side. He plucked a cigar from
his front pocket and used a lighter to light it.

"What are you, some mob boss?" He looked like he
belonged in a movie as he puffed smoke rings in the air.

"Darling, you have no idea what I'm capable of." He
winked and motioned for me to sit next to Izzy.

You don't know what I'm capable of. I glared at him,
trying to figure out what I was capable of. He grabbed a
rope.

"So if you are going to kill us, why? Why did you kill
Alexelrod? What did he ever do to you?" I at least wanted
to know the reasons if I was going to die, and try to stall
him until something, anything came into my head.

"He was all gung ho for Ophelia Biblio to come to town when I told him about her." He moved the cigar to the other side. He took a puff and blew smoke rings in the air. "You see," he pointed at the woman. "Ophelia was never going to leave Colton. And I needed her to make my power potion to release the souls of my friends who had all been banned to live a life of silence as animals."

"You brought the animals here." I wanted to confirm what I had seen in the globes at Mystic Lights.

"Yes. I sent them here after I found out Izzy was looking for an interim sheriff." He spoke with the cigar stuck between his front teeth. "Only she didn't know that I had sent Colton a little message about the position. That way Ophelia would come here and they would bring his mother." He pointed to the woman again.

"You are Colton's mom?" Everything was becoming very clear. "You needed his mom, because she is a Curist, to make you the potion. Then when she made the transition for them, you were planning on taking Whispering Falls over and making it an evil Dark-Sider community?"

"I underestimated you, June Heal." He tapped his temple. "But you didn't figure it out in time. We are one step away from the final cure. Thanks to your little tip about the book." He nodded over to the coffee table where the "Mysteries and Magical Spells" book lay.

Madame Torres's glow from the other room was so intense, Gandolf raised his hands to shield the brightness, dropping the rope.

I grabbed before it landed on the ground and started wrapping it around his ankles. Izzy shoved her bound feet forward and knocked Gandolf on his butt. He flailed his arms trying to get free.

"Hold it right there!" Oscar's voice rang out along with the sound of a shot.

Silence took over, colliding with the smoke of the bullet and the smell of gunpowder.

I must be dead. There was no other way I could have heard Oscar's voice.

"Don't move!"

I opened my eyes. Colton and Oscar were standing there, legs apart, arms stretched out and guns pointed at Gandolf.

Gandolf had stopped flailing when Oscar shot his gun into the air. I was relieved to see that I wasn't dead and that he truly was there.

"Are they okay?" Ophelia ran in and rushed over to Colton's mom. She threw her arms around her before she took the gag out of her mouth.

"I'm fine. Help Izzy," his mom nodded toward us. I sat there in shock.

"I will." I jumped to my feet and reached over to take Izzy's gag off and then untied her hands from behind her back.

"Thank you June." Izzy rotated her wrists a few times before she leaned over and untied her feet. "If it weren't for you, Alise and I would probably be dead."

"Yes, thank you." Alise, Colton's mom, held her hands to her heart. "I didn't want to hurt the community. Colton and Ophelia were so looking forward to moving here."

"So you two are a couple?" Oscar questioned as he handcuffed Gandolf.

"We are." Ophelia hugged Colton, but Colton moved away so he could help Oscar hoist Gandolf to his feet. "But we understand that there can't be two spiritualists in a relationship with separate businesses. Is that right?"

"So," Oscar held Gandolf's cuffs with one hand and gestured between all of us. "This spiritualist thing is real?"

Chapter Thirty

It didn't seem like it was only two weeks ago that the entire fate of Whispering Falls was on the verge of being non-existent, or the fact that Oscar Park didn't know the real me, but fourteen days can seem like a long time when everything was falling into place – well, almost everything.

"I told you that you needed to find a new man." Madame Torres was still going on and on about the Make-Me-A-Match profile she had made unbeknownst to me. Even from the bottom of my bag she was still loud. "It worked for her."

"Just ignore her," I told Ophelia as I blew Madame Torres off while I was waiting for the book club to start.

I had reserved a spot in Ever After Books that was set up for such clubs. I loved how Ophelia complemented the room with big fluffy white couches that had snuggly covers on them to curl up with while everyone got the opportunity to discuss the book. She even had coffee and tea from The Gathering Grove and pastries from Wicked Good.

It was our very first book club meeting and I hated to admit that I never once opened or read "Gone With The Ghost". After all, I had spent all of my free time telling Oscar about our past and his. Besides, I was here mostly for the company and meeting up with friends.

After he rescued us from that terrible Dark-Sider, Gandolf, Izzy said that there were special instances where people can know about us. Since he did save our hinnies, Oscar was definitely considered a special circumstance.

"Don't you wish she had an off button?" Ophelia twirled her finger around and pointed to my bag.

"Sometimes." I winked and patted my bag. "I have to say that she was a big help in solving Alexelrod's murder. I was convinced that you and Colton had something to do with it that night. I was even going to go tell Gandolf, but you know how that turned out, and here we are."

"Yes, here we are." Colton walked up behind us holding a fresh cup of coffee from The Gathering Grove. He wrapped Ophelia in his arms and kissed her on the head. She glowed…literally.

I had to admit that Colton looked devilishly handsome in his new Whispering Falls Sherriff uniform, but not as good as Oscar did.

"What about the amendment to the laws?" Ophelia questioned. "In particular, the one where spiritualist shop owners can't be in a relationship and have two businesses?"

"That's a good question." I had been working with Izzy on how we can update the old spiritual laws. Although the laws were good, sometimes the laws have to grow with the community, and our laws hadn't been changed or tweaked in over one hundred years. "Aunt Helena is very good in the law department, so we'll have a meeting with her, then we will bring it to a village vote."

There was excitement, not only with Colton and Ophelia, but also with Gerald and Petunia and whoever else had a relationship in Whispering Falls. They way I looked at it, if the shop owners were happy, it would show in their stores, and that would bring more business to Whispering Falls.

"How are you and Oscar?" Colton asked.

He had gotten to know Oscar a little better after they took Gandolf into custody. They had even hung out for drinks one night in Locust Grove. Oscar was curious about our gifts and he probably felt more comfortable talking to a man about it.

"We're fine." I smiled. It would take Oscar time to truly understand what all took place over the last few months. "What about you two love birds?"

Madame Torres was right. Make-Me-A-Match got it right when they paired Colton and Ophelia.

"We are great, right honey?" Ophelia turned to face Colton and gave him a peck on the cheek.

"Good afternoon." Eloise strolled in with Petunia following closely behind her.

"Good afternoon." I reached over and tugged on Petunia's sleeve. A chipmunk ran out of the neck of her shirt and nestled right in the crook of her neck. Petunia picked the little brown fury creature up and stuck it in her hair. There were a few shakes and wiggles of the messy updo before the critter settled in. "Have things settled down? How are things?"

"Great!" Petunia clasped her hands together. "Ever since the whole Gandolf thing, and you giving me a power potion reversal for the animals," she gestured toward Alise, Colton's mom. "They have been shipped back to the community out west and are no longer my problem."

Even though the animals were bad souls, I still couldn't believe that Gandolf had meticulously plotted the entire plan. Thank goodness, he was gone forever.

"Tell me, have you talked with Oscar any more about tonight?" Eloise asked with a little hope in her voice.

Since I had been given the all clear to tell Oscar about his past, I also told him that his past included Eloise. He was shocked and elated to find out that he had an aunt still living and loved that she did have pictures to prove it, but sad that he didn't remember her.

Eloise didn't care if he remembered her or not. She only wanted to love him. With a little bit of coaxing, Eloise invited us over for dinner and he agreed to it.

"We will be there by six."

"Oh!" Eloise threw her hands in the air and wrapped them around me, giving me a big bear hug. "I can't stay. I

have to rush home and get things ready. I was sure he
wouldn't agree to it."

Petunia and I stood with our mouths open, as Eloise
didn't waste any time getting the heck out of Ever After
Books and pushing everyone out of her way in the process.

"It looks like it's just you and me kid." Petunia
laughed and plopped down on the one of the couches.

The other members of the book club couldn't make it
because they were still working in their shops. Luckily, I
still had Faith on the payroll and she was able to keep the
paper going and also keep my customers happy.

"Why don't we wait until we can meet at my cottage
some night?" It was hard for me to give up any night
because I wanted to continue to work with Oscar to regain
his memory.

He still had no recollection of us being in love, and I
didn't tell him all of that. I figured that I'd let nature take
its course. If he falls in love with me it will be even better,
because there would be no magic involved…well, no real
magic.

"That sounds like a great idea." Petunia stood back up
and clasped her hands in front of her. "I have a lot of baths
to give today and hair brushing if you would like to help?"
She stretched out her hands.

"Of course I would." I accepted her offer in helping me
up.

Even though Oscar didn't remember us, or our time
here in Whispering Falls, it was okay. I had the best of both
worlds. I had my dearest friends in the world and a best
friend in him.

For Eloise's sake, I did wish that he had some memory
of her.

Chapter Thirty-One

There was no reason to get fancy or even dolled up for Oscar. He still looked at me as a best friend. Wearing my red dress and flat sandals would be perfect for a night at Eloise's. After all, it wasn't about me.

"June, are you ready?" Oscar was still good about letting himself into my house just like he had crawled through my childhood window so many times in Locust Grove.

"Almost." I grabbed Madame Torres off the bedside table and threw her in my bag. The night air could sometimes be a little chilly. The cloak Eloise had given me would be perfect so I plucked it out of my closet before I made my way down the hall.

"You have to be kidding me!" A soft gasp escaped from my lips when I saw Mr. Prince Charming doing his signature figure-eight move around Oscar's feet. It was the first time that I had ever seen him be nice to Oscar.

"I guess someone is starting to come around." Oscar bent down to pick him up.

"I wouldn't do…" I was going to warn him, but it was too late. Mr. Prince Charming was already up in Oscar's arms, nudging him with his nose. "I guess you two are friends?"

Meow, meow. Mr. Prince Charming bounced out of his arms and out of the door that Oscar had left open. There was no way that I was going to see Eloise and make Mr. Prince Charming stay home. He loved her just as much as I did.

"Looks like we are ready and he knows the way." Oscar pointed out the door.

"Yes." I smiled. A feeling like tiny butterflies fluttered in my chest. I shut the door behind us. We followed Mr.

Prince Charming's tail that was dancing in the tall grass just beyond the Gathering Rock into the woods.

"Why does she live so far back in the woods?" Oscar asked.

"Whispering Falls used to be a Good-Sider community, up until recently when I took over as Village President. I believe that everyone can work together." The less information for him to process was probably better for everyone. I knew he would learn all of it soon enough. My intuition told me.

"And I gave all of this up?"

"Yep." I nodded.

"Why?" He asked the million-dollar question that I knew I was going to have to answer sooner rather than later.

"I was in a little pickle." We continued to walk deep into the woods. When we made it to the clearing where Eloise's treehouse sat, I stopped and let Oscar take it in before I finished my story.

"Wow." The amazement on his face was exactly how I had felt when I first saw where she lived. It was the most spectacular house ever. "I've always wanted to have a real treehouse. And that is my aunt's?" A huge grin crossed his face like a little boy who had just caught a foul ball at a baseball game.

"And she's wonderful." I put my hand on his arm for him to stop. He turned to me. His blue eyes were mesmerizing and I wanted nothing more than to kiss him. "About the pickle I was in."

"You must've done something worse than burn down a shed if I was willing to give up an aunt with a treehouse." He joked. There was nothing funny to me about it. If he only knew that I would take back what he did in a heartbeat.

"I was accused of a crime and you weren't allowed to help me." I swallowed. "In fact they took you off the case until the crime was solved."

Something beyond the tree caught my eye. I glanced over and saw the three Marys levitating between the trees. Mary Ellen was in the middle and gestured for me to continue.

"You went to the Elders, which I will explain later, and told them you wanted to be released of all of your powers in order to help me. Only you didn't realize what you were saying and were also stripped of your memory."

"Oh." He didn't flinch, blink, or looked shocked. He just stood there, listening.

"Over the past few months I have been working on a spell to bring you back to me." I threw my hand over my mouth. "I mean back to the spiritual world."

"You and I?" He played finger ping-pong between the two of us.

I nodded my head. My heart soared when I noticed his eyes suddenly fill with a fierce sparkle...almost like *magic*.

A Note From The Author

Thank you so much for reading my novel. I'm truly grateful for the time we have spent together. Reviews are very important to an author's career and I would appreciate it if you could take a couple minutes of your time by clicking on the click below and leaving a review for my novel. Thank you so much, and I hope we continue to meet in the world of books. ~Tonya Kappes

International bestselling author Tonya Kappes spends her day lost in the world of her quirky characters that get into even quirkier situations.

When she isn't writing, she's busy being the princess, queen and jester of her domain, which includes her BFF husband, her teenage guys, two dogs, and one lazy Kitty.

Tonya has an amazing STREET TEAM where she connects with her fans on a daily basis. If you are interested in becoming a Tonya Kappes Street Team member, be sure to message her on Facebook.

For more information, check out Tonya's website, Tonyakappes.com, Facebook, and Twitter.

Made in the USA
Columbia, SC
28 November 2017